TWENTY THIRTY-THREE

JAMES A TURNER

WestBow Press books may be ordered through booksellers or by contacting:

WestBow Press
A Division of Thomas Nelson & Zondervan
1663 Liberty Drive
Bloomington, IN 47403
www.westbowpress.com
1 (866) 928-1240

ISBN: 978-1-4908-2412-3 (sc)
ISBN: 978-1-4908-2413-0 (hc)
ISBN: 978-1-4908-2411-6 (e)

Library of Congress Control Number: 2014901592

Printed in the United States of America.

WestBow Press rev. date: 02/25/2014

Contents

List of Characters

Colonel Roger Barker U.S. Army .... Assistant to President Hall
Willie Barnes........past U.S. speaker of the House of Representatives
Al Biggs .... Fort Worth meteorologist
Robert Bold....................................Texas Speaker of the House
Ginger Brown........................... vice president under Hal Wilson
Buddy...Texas state trooper
Herman Butler...............................U.S. secretary of the treasury
William Carney.................chief justice of the Texas Supreme Court
Neville Crow .... U.S. secretary of defense
Gerald Cunningham .... 47th vice president
Timothy Dawkins ....speaker of the U.S. house of representatives
John Dewey .... renowned secular humanist
Ed .... Captain Smith's partner
Evelyn ....Colonel Baker's fiancée from the past
Glenda .... Colonel Baker's wife
Becky Hall................................ Ellie and Jesse Hall's daughter
Ellie Hall..Jesse's wife
Jesse Hall..........................Texas governor who becomes president
Orville Hall...Jesse's dad
E G Hill ....black activist preacher
Thomas Hardy .... colonel in the Texas Rangers
Pastor Harold Haynes .... Orville's pastor
Paul and Cathy Hines .... members of Orville's Sunday school class
Jim .... friend from Fort Worth
Joe ....barber
Leigh .... Les Mundo's wife

Lenore .... Ellie's mom
Howard Martin ....Texas's attorney general
Les Mundo .... band leader from Ohio
President Oner .... Russian President
Luis Parton .... U.S. attorney general
Edwin Roberts .... director of Texas Department of Public Safety
Clint Ross .... lieutenant governor of Texas
Ruby .... Jesse's secretary while governor
Juanita Salazar ....President Hall's secretary
Robert Schultz .... chairman Joint chief of Staff
Bill Smith .... church member
Captain Smith ....Texas state trooper
Suzy .... waitress at Paris Coffee Shop
Vernon Wiley .... 47th president
Wilma ....Howard Martin's wife
Hal Wilson.. 48th president
Major General John H. Williams.. adjutant general, Texas State Guard
Sherry Wilson .... Timothy Dawkins chief of staff
George and Olivia Yates .... members of Orville's Sunday school class

Chapter 1

Sunday School Party

Friday Night, October 28, 2016

Orville Hall was a bit nervous; he was hosting the First United Methodist Reformed Church annual Sunday school party. Usually thirty or forty people attended this gathering. Each person brought a covered dish, and the host supplied the meat and drinks. For more than twenty years, the party had been held at Orville's house, but this was the first time he had hosted the party alone. Linda, Orville's wife of nearly forty years, had died unexpectedly in January. This year, Jesse, his only son, and his daughter-in-law, Ellie, were going to help serve and clean up. Both Jesse and Ellie knew the guests well.

Usually their pastor would speak briefly, but this year he couldn't attend, so Orville did the sharing. To accommodate this many people, the furniture had been moved to one side of the living room and den, and card tables were set up to hold the food and seat the people. Orville had smoked two large hams and a turkey, which he thought should be enough. Several of the ladies had come early to get everything ready. They probably thought Orville couldn't do it by himself, and they wanted to help. He welcomed the help, which allowed him to greet everyone as they arrived.

Between the dining room and the living room were large French doors; you could see most of the guests from any area. Everyone arrived promptly, visited briefly, and stood together for the food to be blessed.

Orville asked Jesse to offer thanks for the dinner that was about to be served. "Father," Jesse said, "we come together again to fellowship, eat, and return to our homes. We acknowledge You and offer thanks to You as our only God. You provided this great dinner. We confess our great sadness that my mom and Dad's wife, Linda, is not with us today. At the same time we're thankful that she is with You. We pray blessings on this food and on everyone here. I offer this prayer in the name of Jesus Christ, our Lord and only Savior. Amen."

From that moment on, not much was said. Everyone looked sad when Linda's name was mentioned, but once their plates were full, their sadness was replaced with smiles.

After everyone had several helpings and a dessert or two, Orville spoke up. "Folks, tonight I'm privileged to speak in place of Pastor Haynes, and I will do my best to keep your attention and not talk too long." As Orville began to speak, many of the ladies left for the kitchen. Cleaning the kitchen was their excuse for not listening. No sooner had he started to talk than a few guests politely got up from their seats, waved good-bye, and left.

"Tonight I will share how my life changed after Linda passed away. It was last January, almost a year ago. It was so sudden—she just left us. I was a zombie; I would wake up in the middle of the night and drink coffee till daylight. Then I would sit there for hours not knowing what to do next. This went on until sometime in June." As Orville spoke, his lower lip quivered a little. Ellie went to Orville and put her arm around him. Orville wasn't trying to stir up any emotions, but several of the guests had begun to cry. "I'm sorry, I'm very sorry. I didn't want anyone to be upset, but I needed to explain where I was coming from. Anyway, sometime in June, I went to get my hair cut. I was sitting there waiting for my turn and looking for something to read. I found an old copy of a *National Review* magazine. The *National Review* is a very conservative far-right magazine. I don't usually read this type of material, but the cover caught my attention. It read in large print, 'The Four Horsemen of Progressivism,' and in smaller print it read, 'The Men Who Created Our World.' I wanted to see what progressivism was and who these men were. No sooner had I found the article than Joe, my barber, said it was my turn. I kept the magazine and sat in the barber chair for my haircut. I asked Joe if he had read the article. He said he didn't read that political crap. I politely laughed and asked if I could borrow the magazine for a day or two. Joe reached for the magazine and noticed it was several years old. He then said, 'Keep it. It's time for it to be thrown away anyway.'

"I don't know what my fascination was, but I couldn't wait to get home to read the article. I hadn't yet realized that for the first time since January, I was actively doing something. It wasn't much, but it was progress. A few weeks later, I realized that my life had made a turn for the better. I still missed Linda very much, but my life had taken a turn, and I wasn't a zombie any longer.

"It is not easy for me to describe progressivism. It is something that's been here for a long, long time. What I learned from that article caused me to become obsessed with finding what truth really is. I've been a Christian since childhood. It is who I am, and it's what I do. I'm basically a good person. I have made mistakes, I guess many mistakes, but my life is simple, and it keeps on going forward, no matter what. All of that applies to most everyone I know. As we live out our lives, we try to do better as we grow older. The article wasn't about biblical truth, but that's where it quickly led me. It hit me like a ton of bricks. I didn't understand truth, and I thought I knew who Jesus was, but I really didn't understand as much as I thought I did. I was a nice man who went to church regularly, and I thought that was enough." Everyone was used to hearing Orville each Sunday, but this was different; it wasn't his regular message of encouragement.

"Pontius Pilate sent Jesus to His death because of charges made against Him by the Jews. Pilate asked Him if He was a king and what truth was. Jesus answered, 'You say that I am a king. In fact, the reason I was born and came into the world is to testify to the truth. Everyone on the side of truth listens to Me.' 'What is truth?' retorted Pilate. With this he went out again to the Jews gathered there and said, 'I find no basis for a charge against him' [John 18:37–38 ESV]. Jesus said in another place, 'I am the way, and the truth and the life, no one comes to the Father but through me' [John 14:6]." Orville went on to say, "We may not fully understand what truth is, but this is the place to start our search, through Jesus Christ and in the holy Bible. My understanding of truth is that it is everything said by Jesus, it is who He is, and if we know Him, we can understand truth. It's not a complicated word, but nowadays most people and many churches aren't searching for truth."

Orville then said, "Next I'll read from the *Stanford Encyclopedia of Philosophy*, published Tuesday, June 13, 2006. I quote, 'Truth is one of the central subjects in philosophy. It is also one of the largest. Truth has been a topic of discussion in its own right for thousands of years. Moreover, a huge variety of issues in philosophy relate to truth, either by relying on theses about truth, or implying theses about truth.' End of quote. The great colleges and universities of our land and throughout the world have searched for their meaning of truth. They have made their own interpretation of what truth is without even considering what God's truth is. Without knowing God they can't possibly understand what truth really is. They teach our young what their understanding of truth is, not God's. This has gone on since the fall of man." Several of the ladies came from the kitchen, and without saying a word, their husbands stood up, waved good-bye, and quietly went toward the door, their wives close behind them. Now there were only ten people left to hear Orville's passionate story; half were very interested, and the other half were being polite.

Orville continued as if he didn't notice that most of the dinner guests were now gone. Jesse and Ellie were left to finish cleaning the kitchen by themselves. "Soon after reading several articles and doing some research on my own, I discovered a simple truth. The answer to what truth is, its that there is only one truth. You do not have to be smart to know what truth is. It only matters that you belong to God and really want to know what truth really is. Truth is imparted to us by God if we seek Him. It's that simple, and He is the only way for a person to understand truth.

"Folks, that was part one of my story for you this evening. The other part is that I finally came to understand something that's bothered me for years. Next month we will vote for a new president. Have you ever wondered how a person who goes to church with you every week, a respected deacon in your church, a person who believes in God the same as you do, would be for abortion, forbidding school prayer, and homosexual marriage? This is my dilemma: we have basically two political parties, the Democrats and the Republicans. Both parties have Christians and non-Christians in them. It would seem to me that the Christians would always vote the same way. Their vote would always be influenced by God's Word, truth.

"Many years ago abortion became legal; now unborn humans are being killed by the millions. Prayer in school was eliminated. Same-sex marriage became normal. Over time being a Christian wasn't a popular choice for most of America. These issues defined each political party. The Democrats chose what they called a woman's right to choose: the one pregnant with a human baby could now choose to abort or not. Freedom of religion was used to expel prayers from school. If a man and woman could marry, why not two men marrying, and why not two women marrying? Fair is fair, and love is love. Also, it is very scary, but the government has started to decide who gets medical treatment and who doesn't. I am afraid of what has started to happen to our seniors, especially since I am one of them. It's been kept out of the news by the news services, but medical care is being determined by a government-directed board, and now some are left to die because of the common good for everyone.

"Over time a Christian's freedom to obey God became a private, personal issue and a privilege and should not hinder society from advancing the common good of all its citizens. The American citizen's rights and freedoms are upheld by the Supreme Court. Man's rights given by man supersede what God has told us in His Word. A political party, the Supreme Court, and most Americans have gone their own way. It is the natural course of man in these times.

"America was founded on the principle of freedom of religion. Anyone could believe however they wanted to, or not believe. A government can't mandate what is in a person's heart. America wasn't created as a Christian nation, dedicated to God, as most of us have always thought.

The phrase 'One Nation Under God' was started in 1954. 'In God We Trust' was started in 1956. The founding fathers were good, decent men, but most weren't recognized as great men of faith, just great men. In my quest for answers I couldn't find one of our founding fathers who professed serving God and seeking His truth as the solution to our young nation's problems.

"So here we have a nation with several kinds of people living together in peace. Unbelievers, people of other, non-Christian faiths, Christian people who aren't committed to truth, and a small minority who are faithful believers or orthodox Christians. What is noteworthy is that in many orthodox churches not all are truth seekers. In many non-orthodox churches there are some truth seekers.

"From all that I have just said, there is only one conclusion. It is simply and only what is truth. Pilate didn't understand, and executed Jesus Christ. Truth has slipped from America, and millions of infants are legally slaughtered. We forbid prayers in school to keep from being convicted of our ways.

"A few years ago in Austin they started a university, the John Dewey University of Philosophical and Theological Studies. Here man's rational interpretation of truth and God's unchanging truths are combined by mere men for the well-being of all men. Since America comprises many types, this will accommodate everyone, or most everyone. The only groups left out would be the small orthodox Christian group, and other faiths that actually practiced their beliefs. These may not necessarily be groups, but individuals who believe and know God. This small minority of believers are really disenfranchised, as the Bible says they should be. Man can finally distribute equality for all, and rule the day for the good of all. Man has exalted himself as higher than God. He doesn't realize this; if he knew of his actions and intent, he would be able to know God. Then perhaps he would confess and repent. The devil has kept this secret from his minions by using their intellect and pride against them unaware.

"This would seem to be a great problem for the many great men of our times who are only seeking justice for everyone in an equal society.

This was easily solved as time passed. Abortion, school prayers, and homosexuals having the same rights of marriage became great issues. Many of the people in the different groups didn't have a problem with equal rights for everyone. The orthodox Christians and other faiths saw this as contrary to their beliefs. They saw this as eroding family structure and weakening society, and mainly an affront to God and His Word. In other words one truth must be accepted and another truth set aside. This is what the university is about. This is what most universities and colleges are about—a truth that works for all like-minded people.

"The debate began a long time ago. If a person's sacred faith would deny freedom and liberty to a group or a person, then that person's faith was not acceptable in an equal society, where all are equal, where all have the same rights. America has evolved to a place where its own truth must be the way for all, a better way, with a common good, and equality for everyone. This has resulted in Christians and practitioners of other faiths becoming the enemies of a new society. This allows a true separation of people of faith, or church and state. This problem is naturally taking care of itself. I will close with these Scriptures:

"'Go to this people and say, "You will be ever hearing but never understanding; For this people's heart has become calloused; they hardly hear with their ears, and they have closed their eyes. Otherwise they might see with their eyes, hear with their ears, understand with their hearts and turn, and I would heal them"' [Acts 28:26–27]."

Before Orville could close out the evening, Mrs. Yates waved her hand in the air to show that she had something to say. Orville acknowledged her and said, "Yes, Olivia, it is your turn."

George Yates, Olivia's husband, looked a little embarrassed. He could sense from his wife's body language that she didn't approve of everything Orville had said. She started by saying, "Orville, I've been coming to your Sunday school class for years, and for the most part I've enjoyed listening to you. Tonight I feel like you took our university out of context and also the great colleges and universities in America. There needs to be a way to bridge the gap in understanding. That is what these institutions are doing. And I think you spoke of God's church in a negative light." With that she stood up, and George followed her out the door.

Orville didn't look surprised by her remarks and calmly said, "Let's pray." By now the kitchen was cleaned and Jesse and Ellie had joined the group. "Father, our understanding can only be seen through Your eyes, and if we are to know truth, it is from You only. That is my only prayer tonight. Father, open our eyes to Your truth. In Jesus' name I do pray. Amen."

Chapter 2

Orville and the Church

Sunday, October 30, 2016

Orville was prepared as usual for his Sunday school class. It was almost nine thirty, and only five people had showed up. Somehow he had expected this. Last Friday most of the class had left before he was finished with his talk, but he knew everyone was aware of what he had said. As he waited for any stragglers, he knew that the church would have issues with his point of view. There was more to come because of what he'd said at his house on Friday. One more couple took their seats. Orville thought, *Seven—not too bad. We will continue with our class.*

"Good morning, everyone. As we can see, many can't be here today, but we will do our best without them. Before I pray, I would like to mention last Friday at my house. I spoke about current events, both political and spiritual. Apparently some took issue with what was said. I won't try to defend myself: truth is truth. Let's pray and go from there. Father, we live in a complicated world. Sadly our culture usually dictates our view on life. If we were raised to believe one way and our society is going another, what should we do? Father, we should look to You for answers. That isn't our only choice, but it's the only correct one. Father, I see dark days ahead, and I pray that we look to You for guidance, peace, strength, and answers. I pray in the name of Jesus Christ, our Lord and Savior, amen.

"Well, folks, I had a lesson prepared, but I will put it aside and allow the Holy Spirit to give us a lesson today." Orville sat still and everyone else remained quiet as well. After a minute or more Orville said, "The last few months have been the worst and best in my life. As you know, I had a very hard time coping with the loss of Linda. When it seemed to be at its worst, something happened to make everything worthwhile. I appreciate that during the first six months of our loss everybody pitched in and we still had our Sunday school class. During that time in my life I don't think I opened the Bible one time.

"I think this is what happened to me. When God does something, you are left with the choice to think you did it or He did it. If you think you did it, you will have to learn your lesson again. If you know He was the one, then you get a get-out-of-jail-free card, and you will continue on." Some laughed at Orville's attempt at humor; some sat still and showed no response. Orville thought to himself, *Here we go again: the truth is killing me.* "Anyway," Orville continued, "we don't all have the same sense of humor, but I will continue on and try not to be too funny." Some smiled and some didn't, and Orville continued.

"Of all the many Holy Scriptures, three verses are my favorite. I'm not discounting John 3:16 and other Scriptures we know and learned from our youth. But I chose these three verses years ago. I would say them in conversation and use them in prayer. As I discovered these verses, I memorized them. I thought they were a part of me. Galatians 2:20 says, 'I have been crucified with Christ and I no longer live, but Christ lives in me. The life I now live in the body, I live by faith in the Son of God, who loved me and gave himself for me.' The second is Matthew 6:33: 'but seek first his kingdom and his righteousness, and all these things will be given to you as well.' Last but not least by any means is John 8:31–32: 'To the Jews who had believed him, Jesus said, "If you hold to my teaching, you are really my disciples. Then you will know the truth, and the truth will set you free."' A point I will make is that before John 8:31, the Bible says, 'As He was saying these things many believed in Him.' After John 8:31 and 32 it says in verse 33, 'They answered him, "We are Abraham's descendants and have never been slaves of anyone. How can you say that we shall be set free?'" Back then some who heard believed, and as we read, some didn't or couldn't. Today is no different. Somehow God allowed me to believe and understand 'truth,' a very simple word *truth.* As I began to grasp this word, I began to notice drastic changes in my life. I realized that God speaks to me. I can hear Him, and we talk. It is amazing; it has completely changed my life. Another result was a deep, great interest in Jesus being crucified and dying on the cross. It became very intimate and very personal. It seems as if now I have deep feelings from another place in my being."

Paul Hines, one of the people in the Sunday school class who had failed to laugh at Orville's attempt at humor, spoke up. With a slight smirk on his face he said, "Orville, are you trying to say that you and God have conversations?"

Orville kindly looked at both Paul and his wife, Cathy, who was joining him with a slight smirk on her face. He replied, "First before answering your question, are you attempting to be funny at my expense?" Then Orville continued without giving them a chance to answer. "I'll read from John 10," and he slowly read the complete chapter with sincerity and humbleness. As he read the Scriptures, the words touched his heart and he momentarily lost his composure. Paul and Cathy's smirks had long left their faces. Both were unashamedly crying. There was something happening in this Sunday school class that had never happened before.

As the class neared its end, a church usher came in to give Orville a note. He knew what was in the note before he opened it. After the class was empty, he read the note.

> *Dear Brother Hall,*
>
> *If you have time today, could you drop by my office for a chat, immediately after the morning service? I won't keep you very long.*
>
> *Thanks*
> *Pastor Haynes*

Church promptly concluded at eleven forty-five. Pastor Haynes took his place near the front door so he could shake the church members' hands as they left the church. Orville walked down the aisle to shake the pastor's hand as he had done for many years. Pastor Haynes's smile left him momentarily as he shook Orville's hand. "Orville, please wait for me. I will be in my office in five minutes. Go on in and have a seat."

As Pastor Haynes entered the church office area and went into his private office, he said, "Come on in" to Orville, who was sitting in a chair outside the pastor's office. As the pastor was going toward his seat, he took off his black robe. As they both entered the room and sat down, Orville felt like a student going into the principal's office for some offense he had just committed. He could sense a different tone coming from the pastor.

"Orville, Saturday when I got back in town, I had several calls from members of your Sunday school class. Several families were very upset with some of the things you said. If it had been only one or two, it might have been just a misunderstanding. Orville, you've served at this church for years, and this is the first complaint about you. I'm very disappointed in what was said Friday night." As the pastor spoke, Orville knew he wouldn't let him defend himself, and he felt like he didn't need to. "Orville, since your wife died—"

Orville interrupted the pastor. "Sir, my wife's name is Linda. It's much too soon to forget her name."

Pastor Haynes's face turned red and he said, "Orville, I'm so sorry. I do remember Linda's name, and she is missed very much. Let's continue on. We have many members from John Dewey University. Some are what you call homosexuals. These people faithfully serve in this church and the community. If they hear what you said Friday night, it could be extremely harmful to our mission and their well-being. I hope you will be more considerate of others in what you say in the future. That is all I have to say about Friday night. As far as I'm concerned, that's the end of that topic.

"I do have another matter to discuss with you. I have decided to make a few changes in the way we present our Sunday school classes.

What we're doing is inviting the graduating seniors from John Dewey to co-teach with our regular teachers. This means that you will have a co-teacher to share your duties with."

Orville had expected something, but not this. "Whose idea was this?" he asked.

Pastor Haynes replied with a tone of authority, "All ministers, teachers, and office staff are my responsibility."

Orville then asked, "Can the student teacher start Sunday?"

The pastor replied, "Yes, that's the plan."

Orville said, "Well, that just about covers it," and he stood up to leave. "One more thing: last Friday I had a pocket recorder, and I recorded the meeting. Also on the tape is today's Sunday school class. You may want to listen to this."

The pastor looked annoyed, and said, "No, Orville. The matter is closed." Orville laid the tape on the pastor's desk and said, "You need to hear this tape." Neither one of the men offered to shake hands, and Orville walked out of the pastor's study, leaving the tape and the pastor behind with a bewildered look on the latter's face.

Chapter 3

Orville Meets Timmy

Friday Morning, September 15, 2017

Orville heard something outside his house that sounded different from the usual chickens, his old cow, or the goat letting him know they were ready to eat. As he was pouring his first cup of coffee, planning to sit in the old swing on his front porch, he could hear a faint whimpering. He thought it could be any number of animals or birds out here in the country.

As he opened the front door, the noise stopped. Soon Orville was deep in his thoughts and the noise he had heard earlier had left his mind. It was still very early in the morning, and so dark that Orville could see two small eyes in the driveway, reflecting the light in the house. *Hmm. Is it a cat? A dog? I guess I'll find out soon enough.* The eyes maintained their distance, and Orville became engrossed in his own deep thoughts again.

It was now barely daybreak, and Orville could see a small dog sitting in the driveway about seventy-five feet from where he sat. *Well, I guess I have another stray dog to feed,* he thought to himself. *In all the years I've lived here, I bet I've had fifty or so dogs.*

I raise them just for the coyotes to eat. If they would stay inside at night, they might live a little longer, but most of the dogs that find me can't be brought into the house anyway.

Here I am almost seventy-five years old and my main purpose in life is to sit and drink coffee by myself and raise stray dogs for coyotes to eat. They try to get my chickens, but I lock them up in their pen at night.

By now the dog was about twenty feet from the porch, and Orville could see he had missed several meals. "Wait here, pooch. I'll find you a piece of bologna or something." The dog maintained his distance while his adopted master went to get him some much-needed food. Soon Orville returned with a package of sliced bologna, just what the dog had ordered. Orville took one slice and placed it at the bottom of the porch steps. That was a lot closer than the dog wanted to be. Knowing this, Orville took his place in the swing, drank his coffee, and watched his friend decide what to do. Speaking out loud Orville said, "I think his name shall be Timmy. Yes, Timmy is a good name for a dog."

Orville thought the dog could be thirsty. *Maybe I should get him some water to drink.* No sooner had the door closed behind Orville than the dog grabbed the bologna slice and was on his way. Orville returned with water and set it at the top of the steps with another piece of bologna. He returned to his coffee and waited. By now it was light enough to read, and he started to read the morning newspaper, seemingly ignoring the dog hiding in the shrubs. The dog crawled low to the ground as if to keep from being seen; then once he was within a few feet of the porch, he made a dash for the slice of bologna. This went on for several slices of lunch meat. When the package was nearly empty, the dog wagged his tail slightly. He had found a home, a home that served bologna on the front porch. By now it was nearly seven thirty and time for Orville to start his chores. The chickens needed to be fed, the one cow was hungry, and so was the goat.

Life in the country was simple. After he had done the chores, it was time for a glass of iced tea. No sooner had Orville taken his seat in the swing than a car turned into his driveway. He didn't recognize the lone man in the car. It looked somewhat like Pastor Haynes from church. As the man exited his car, Orville saw that it was the pastor, but he looked different. He had lost a few pounds and had a beard. The dog barked at the pastor as if he were the dog in residence.

As Pastor Haynes approached the top of the steps, he said, "Orville, I came over to ask your forgiveness. After our meeting last October, you never came back to church. At first I was glad. I had this idea—or should I say scheme—to replace the teachers and leaders with my own people. I decided to cast out men I had known for many years. It was easier than I could have expected. Most of the men did just like you: they just left. A couple of leaders—do you remember George Yates and Bill Smith?—they didn't go so easily, but by the time I got to them, I had so many of my new leaders in place that it was futile for anyone to cross me.

"This is what happened: George and Bill both came to see me at the same time, in August. George remembered what you said at your house last October, and it started eating at his conscience. He and Olivia had a change of heart. They felt bad about you leaving the church because of them. George shared with Bill some of the remarks you made in your meeting. Eventually both families left the church. My plan was working; at least I thought it was.

"A few days ago something told me to listen to the tape you gave me. After first hearing it I left early for home and listened to it several more times. I knew then that everything I was doing was wrong. Everything this church was doing was wrong. I took a week off to pray about my dilemma. Actually it wasn't a dilemma; somehow I saw something I had never understood before. After that week I knew what needed to be done. Last Friday I resigned from the church. I left the church. I don't know what's next, but I am very excited about what's happening. So here I am, asking for you to forgive me and at the same time thanking you for the tape."

Orville said, "Of course I forgive you, Pastor. What good news you have brought me today. Well, my dear friend, can I get you a glass of iced tea?"

"Yes, please, but don't call me pastor anymore. Just call me Harold, I suspect we will be talking a lot in the coming months."

Orville said, "Do you want to come in, or would you rather sit outside?"

"Outside is good," Harold said. "This is very good."

After a little small talk and a glass or two of tea, Harold said, "Orville do you mind if I copy the tape you gave me? I would like to send it to a few of my friends, some friends who have gone in the same direction I did. Maybe it could help them. I hope so. Also, I'm thinking about writing a small book about your tape and what you said at your Sunday school party—perhaps forty or fifty pages. I will call it *The Salvation of Pastor Haynes.*"

Chapter 4

For the Good of the People

Year 2032

Totalitarianism (or totalitarian rule) refers to authoritarian political systems where the state recognizes no limits to its authority and strives to regulate every aspect of public and private life wherever feasible. Totalitarian regimes stay in political power through all-encompassing propaganda campaigns disseminated through the state-controlled mass media, use of a single party usually defined by political repression, personality cultism, control over the economy, regulation and restriction of speech, mass surveillance, and widespread use of terror.

—Wikipedia, http://en.wikiquote.org/wiki/Totalitarianism

In the Bible it says something like this: "My sheep hear my voice, and follow me." John 10:27 ESV

Perhaps we were created to follow. Perhaps we were meant to be a simple people, designed to follow Jesus or the devil. Some of the millions upon millions were engineers, many were doctors, and there were cooks, truck drivers, housewives, and all manner of Americans. They were a simple people who blindly followed year after year until it was much too late; then they were led and blindly did as told.

Twenty years ago, liberals running for political office would never be identified publicly as liberals; they would call themselves Democrats.

They weren't Democrats in the original vein of what was long ago called Democrats. They were progressives. Very seldom was this word used by a person running for political office; politically it was too risky. Gradually it was misused to describe a better way for all the people of America, a "new way for all." Over time most everybody was convinced we could all be the same, and everyone could have the same advantages and benefits. This was supposed to be a good thing. Over time *progressivism* became a common word spoken freely. Everyone knew the full meaning of progressivism. Most loathe what this system of government has brought to America. The rulers now freely use the term *progressive* as a way of telling us with great disdain that the "State of America" is who we now are. Long ago the Constitution of the United States of America was disregarded for political convenience. This was done for the "greater good" for all the population, a term that now creates in the masses a fear never felt before in America. Entrepreneurship is nonexistent. Individualism is considered a character fault. Individualism in young children is noticed in schools and dealt with. Every aspect of a past great society has changed to reflect new ideals that promote unified thinking.

Eventually everyone became enslaved to the "state" by buying into an ancient philosophy, one that was thought out and established during the great Enlightenment period. Great thinkers defined truth as the agreed-upon consensus of the majority, or truth originated as needed from the leaders who rule, for the sole purpose of the "greater good." This ultimately allowed a few chosen men with an assumed self-righteousness to rule with their established dignity, for the good of all, just as they saw fit, through their own deceived eyes and as their dark heart guided them.

As America grew older, the churches became seemingly irrelevant. All of the great mega churches were closed by 2022. In twenty twenty-two it was estimated that only about 2 percent of the people attended church regularly; now the people that attend church is much, much smaller. The people who attended church were much different from the church people of the past. Most of the remaining believers still believed in God and the way America should be. It was as if they were standing in place, waiting for orders from God to take America from the godless few who were holding them in a tight grip. It was a fist from Satan with only one objective: to enslave the world to an emptiness that was put into effect at the same time Adam and Eve gained their knowledge of good and evil.

It is the same plan that Hitler used. Hitler dominated Austria in 1938. Not by war; the people came to him by their own choice. It seemed to be the best way at the time for a simple people who followed without knowing truth. If America had not existed in 1938, no one could have stopped the forces of evil during that horrible time in world history. Hitler could have taken over the world. This time it was different. There was no war, it had been very gradual, and we were just like the people of Austria in 1938. No one protested. We all followed, because they fed us and we were afraid of going hungry.

There seemed to be a great but gradual political change in America that started in the 1960s. Environmentalists started appearing on the scene. Many scientists first believed we were having global cooling; they thought that by the time the century ended, we would all freeze to death or earth would become uninhabitable because of the cooling off. This never took place, and as the idea died, scientists began to believe we were really in a global warming period. They decided that the ozone layer that protected us was being rapidly depleted and we were going in the opposite direction. Mother Earth was getting warmer, and there was no return—that is, unless government-regulated mandates were followed; then we might have a chance.

Carbon dioxide is what humans breathe out after inhaling oxygen. We inhale oxygen and make carbon dioxide. Green plants make oxygen. They must have us for survival, and we must have them for survival. This is something God did for the green plants and something He did for us at the time of creation. The environmentalists claimed that global warming was caused by too much carbon in the atmosphere. The theory was never proven scientifically, but was accepted and used by men with evil intentions to change the world's economy and take control of people's lives, to take control of a world filled with simple people who follow. Many other great, recognized leading scientists debunked these theories; they were all ignored. All that was needed was to not recognize any opposition, but to convince the masses of this great lie. This enabled the progressive government backed by the unanimous support of the United Nations to begin a mandate to enforce environmental regulations. A "cap and trade" mandate was created; this was a tax imposed on businesses and individuals for generating too many carbon emissions. From this mandate a surtax was forced on America. Now trees had to be planted and nurtured at great expense to offset the carbon emissions that evil man had supposedly generated.

Global warming empowered the Environmental Protection Agency (EPA). Global warming was the biggest weapon used by the progressives to gain control of America and lead us into totalitarianism. Progressivism was the way, and totalitarianism was the desired result. The US Constitution says that all laws must be passed by Congress. From the beginning the EPA would be empowered by presidential executive order and given a mandate to protect our environment, always for the greater good. The lasting results of the enforced mandates were that gas prices got higher and higher, federal government restrictions on drilling oil and gas increased dramatically, and eventually all the refineries in America were forced to shut down. The EPA completely stopped the mining of coal; it was impossible to get a government permit for a nuclear electrical-generating power plant or coal-fired electrical-generating plant. It was nearly impossible for the automobile manufacturing companies to comply with all the federal government's mandates for better fuel economy and safer air to breathe. Meeting the standards set by the EPA required much more expensive vehicles to be manufactured. In nearly thirty-two years, from 2000 to 2032, America and Europe fell from greatness to orchestrated chaos.

In America by 2021, very few cars were being made, they were very expensive, and very few people could afford one. Not only that, but they were battery powered, and battery-powered automobiles couldn't go very far on a charge. Electricity for home use was regulated with strong government mandates, which usually prohibited owning a car. This made it impossible for the average person to have a car. The average American by 2021 was much different from the average American ten years earlier. By 2025 there weren't distinct classes of American citizens anymore. Because the middle and upper classes had been effectively eliminated, you couldn't call lower-income Americans a lower class of people anymore. Without more than one class of people, everyone was the same, by design.

It wasn't just one political party that created this gradual, horrific, worldwide situation for the governed man. The Democrats in America didn't go rogue all of a sudden. It was a force of unified unconscious but purposeful collective thinking. It was man at his worst. Long ago man became centered on a philosophical idealistic, enlightened mind. Gradually God was cast aside and man was left to go his own way, a way governed by mandates and collective choices. Everyone eventually went in the same insane direction; willing or not, they went. The few in power knew and believed a new way was in order; it was needed, for the good of mankind. Now all the people were finally the same, as planned. The old way of life was destroyed; man's God-given liberty was stolen. Did the leaders really believe it would be in the best interests of the world's weak and poor, or did they plan a new form of serfdom? Their intentions were motivated by their great intellects. For minds that were taught ancient philosophy from childhood, any opposition was met with overwhelming force that no one person or group of people could stand against. The way of past rulers did not rely on men with guns. Eventually all would follow and do as expected: if you fed a dog, he would be your pet. It was once said, but had now been proved, that when the wealthy were gone, all that would be left were slaves.

Chapter 5

The Plan

Friday, November 6, 2032

Jesse Hall, the governor of Texas, was well on his way to his small farm outside Austin. Jesse's dad, Orville, was waiting for him at the farm they shared. The farm was in Dripping Springs, a small community thirty-five miles west of Austin, and was where Governor Jesse grew up. Not much had changed. His mother had died several earlier, and although Orville was nearly ninety, he still took care of the farm. It was a farm in name only. They grew only enough tomatoes and okra for their own consumption. They had one old cow, a goat, and a few chickens, plus sometimes a dog or two; they were all part of the family.

Usually the governor's wife, Ellie, and daughter, Becky, accompanied the governor to the "Alamo." This wasn't the real, famous Alamo, but as a child, Jesse often played Davy Crockett and called his home the Alamo, and the name stuck. Both Ellie and Becky were in San Antonio staying with Ellie's sick mom, Lenore. Lenore wasn't sick physically, but her husband of forty-nine years, Bill, had recently passed, and Lenore now stayed in her bed most of the time. Both Ellie and Becky decided to stay till Mama Lenore went to dinner with them and managed at least one of her recently forgotten big smiles. They secretly hoped to bring her back to Austin for a visit.

The times that the governor and his family spent together at the Alamo were always their happiest. This is where he could relax briefly and not be the governor of Texas for a short while. There were many decisions that Governor Hall needed to make, decisions that could change the direction of Texas and maybe the whole country.

It was getting late in the evening, and the governor drove to the farm on his old 1979 Harley.His father had used the Harley when he was a motorcycle policeman for the City of Austin many years earlier. The Texas Department of Public Safety had the responsibility of protecting Governor Hall, but this time he had just left. He knew he would soon be found out, but he needed a break from the normal entourage of troopers. Usually he conferred with security before leaving the governor's mansion. Each week a schedule was turned in, and everyone knew what activities were to take place.

It was starting to get dark and he hadn't quite reached the Highway 290 cutoff when he heard a familiar siren and saw the flashing lights. The governor's helicopter was hovering about three hundred feet overhead. He pulled over as a black SUV with two troopers inside caught up with him. With lights flashing and the sirens screaming, the troopers slowly exited the SUV and approached the governor. As this was taking place, two Austin capital police vehicles also approached with their sirens screaming and lights flashing. Six very serious men were now standing before the governor as he removed his helmet. Addressing the leader, Governor Hall said, "Ray, Captain Smith, would you all mind turning off your sirens and lights, please?"

Upon seeing that it was the governor, Captain Smith saluted him, saying, "Sir, I wanted to make sure it was you on your motorcycle." Without smiling the captain turned to the five other troopers and said, "Men, it's the governor. I don't think we have a problem after all." Governor Hall was standing in the middle of three vehicles, and it was a very uncomfortable situation that he had just caused. With their lights flashing and sirens on, he knew to let the troopers have their way with him. He had done wrong, and the troopers were going to make a statement. It seemed like a full minute of agonizing noise and flashing lights before Captain Smith looked satisfied and said to the four troopers in two other vehicles,

"Okay, guys, you're not needed. Everything is under control." His partner Ed went to their SUV, turned off the siren and lights, and stood by the driver's side door as the other troopers left the scene.

Governor Hall looked at the captain and said, "Ray, I'm sorry. I should have told you my plans. This will never happen again."

Captain Smith replied in a serious tone, as he always did, "Sir, we will continue with you. Are you headed for the Alamo?" It was probably out of protocol, but Captain Smith stayed at a good distance behind so the governor could enjoy his ride. Governor Hall didn't notice the colorful late-autumn beauty as he made his way to the Alamo.

The farmhouse sat back about three hundred feet from the main road, almost hidden by large pecan trees. By the time they arrived, Captain Smith had alerted security for the governor at the Alamo. Next to the driveway inside the property were temporary quarters for the security detail in what Texans called a double-wide. The governor slowed down enough at the gate so Buddy, the gatekeeper, could identify him. As Jesse went up the front porch steps, he could see the helicopter heading back. Just as the governor reached for the door, his dad opened it and kissed his son on the forehead, just as he had done all his life.

"Are you hungry, son? I fixed some red beans and pork chops, with jalapeno corn bread."

"No, Dad, I'm not hungry, not just yet. Maybe later. What I need is some real good advice."

Orville's smile left his face, and he asked, "Son, is anything wrong?"

Jesse replied, "Dad, how about making a pot of coffee and let's go to the den and talk."

"Sure. I'll get right on it, son," Orville said with a concerned look on his face.

By the time Orville served coffee, the governor was seated in the den with his comfortable old clothes on. He knew he was going to have a long talk with his most trusted adviser. Both sat down for a meeting that could change the course of Texas and a failed America.

"Dad, this is it," Governor Hall said. "The progressives have ruined America. The progressives have been in office ever since George Bush was president. Dad, I have a plan. I told Ellie, Clint, and Howard, but I wanted to run it by you for your approval before we acted." Orville looked interested, but in his heart he sincerely believed this was the beginning of the very last days, which had been prophesied by many biblical prophets, including Jesus Christ.

Orville rubbed his gray, whiskered face and replied, Son I hope your plan works. "Think about this, Dad," Jesse said with noticeable excitement in his voice. "These changes have been coming gradually. Over many years America has been told that we must go to another source of energy. Enough people believed this lie, and the progressives usually have their way. They never let up till they have their way—never. In the last sixty years manufacturing has just about completely stopped. Now only unreliable battery-powered vehicles are being manufactured. These are cars that aren't worth buying, even if you had enough money. The plan was for most everyone to rely on the government in some way. This would give the government more control, resulting in government staying in power indefinitely. Before these gradual changes, America was all about the strength of the people. That was what made us a great nation. Now the people are weak, and it's about any help a person can get from the federal government. Today I believe America has enslaved the whole country without firing a single shot. In 1938 Austria gave itself to Hitler. It wasn't until 1955 that Austria regained its sovereignty. I remember you saying that years ago, and I haven't forgotten it.

"Dad, I can tell everyone about biblical truths, but a blinded populace won't really understand. Or I can tell everyone about the ultimate purpose of a progressive government. Either way it will end up in a political war, and ultimately we will lose as always. Over the last sixty years many have told the truth, but America still did as Austria did: they blindly chose slavery.

"Dad, I've never talked to you or anyone else about being the governor of Texas. I've never had political ambitions. Somehow over a series of events it just happened. I don't like being governor, and I look forward to being out of office."

Orville looked directly into Jesse's eyes and said, "I kind of thought so. You don't fit the mold."

Jesse said, "After graduating from law school, I thought seriously about going to seminary and becoming a pastor in a small church. Now I'm the governor of a state that is just barely hanging on.

"I hope you had your nap today. This may take a while," Jesse said, looking at his dad as Orville rubbed his eyes.

"I'm fine, son. I just have allergies," Orville replied.

"I just heard this afternoon that the Supreme Court will decide Monday who gets to be president," Jesse said. "The election didn't really matter. I really believe Texas needs to provide her own solution to Texas's problems; it's the only way. I don't know where it will lead, but we must act soon. Before the election last Tuesday, we had a plan that just might work. Now our plan has to work.

"The plan is simply to take back America gradually without telling anyone." Jesse's voice rose a bit. "First Texas will have a world global warming summit in Austin as soon as possible. There will be seven scientists to provide evidence of global warming and seven on the opposite side to analyze whatever evidence they present. Only one question will be asked of the first panel: what irrefutable evidence is there for global warming? Only proven scientific evidence will be accepted and considered. With the political history of global warming, I don't think the case can be made for continuing this fiasco.

"Both panels will have thirty days to complete their debate. All the final results will be examined and turned over to a special committee. A four-member council made up from the fourteen scientists will present its findings; two will be chosen from each side. They will work with lawyers to prove or disprove their case before the Texas Supreme Court. The Supreme Court will then have fifteen days to conclude their findings. If for some reason the global warming side fails to convince the court, then that will be a win for the state of Texas. The federal government has strangled America to death without proof; we must have definitive proof to squelch the progressive status quo. If we win, then Texas will immediately make drastic changes in how we operate as a state.

"These changes will be made by executive order, and by the Texas Recovery Mandate, a small group of leaders who are private citizens and understand what real truth is. These are people who won't personally profit by their decisions. It is important to implement change and stop the federal government's control as soon as we can. Our actions will probably cause many other issues to need attention.

"One idea that came across my mind is that as we implement these changes, the federal government will come at us with both barrels. All of Europe is subject to the United Nations, as is almost every country in the world. The only way we will be able to win is to declare that the Declaration of Independence and the Constitution of the United States of America will be revisited, studied, and followed. Our founding fathers understood that the hand of God wrote these documents. These are the same documents we will uphold and serve. These time-proven documents have been set aside and declared ineffective. Laws were changed for the convenience of a few to control the people of America.

"Dad, in the Bible it specifically talks about the purpose of the law, the law that God gave the Israelites. Listen to this: Joshua 1:8 says 'Do not let this Book of the Law depart from your mouth; meditate on it day and night, so that you may be careful to do everything written in it. Then you will be prosperous and successful.' For many years not just our leaders but our citizens let a government take control of every aspect of their lives. They disregarded God. Over time He became irrelevant. They disobeyed God and followed man. These men changed the meaning of the word *truth* for a lie to enslave the population. Without knowing God, a person can't understand what truth really is.

"Next week the lieutenant governor and I will have a long talk. Clint will support me; many of these ideas are his and Howard's. Over the last few years we've become very close and had many late-night discussions. Clint probably knows what I am already thinking because he probably has the same thoughts.

"It's such a simple plan. It will turn the world upside down. The world was turned upside down when the founding fathers declared independence. Some didn't want change, but freedom won out.

"Do you remember LBJ as president? Remember the Great Society? Every person who wanted to could get some kind of government relief. The political purpose was to keep the Democrats in power. This was more than likely what set the stage for what's happened in America today. The result was that America went into great debt, and to this day a great majority of the black population will always vote Democrat. Even today they still vote blindly without really understanding the real issues, and most are churchgoers. This is how the progressives took over America. Dad, studies have shown the result of LBJ's progressive movement: the black people were held back. LBJ enslaved a segment of America, and they went willingly.

"It's getting late and I know you're tired. I've spoken my mind. Let's turn in."

"Okay, son, but I want to say something that's been on my mind." Orville had quietly listened to Jesse, and now it was his turn to speak. This was what Jesse wanted to hear. Orville was sitting at attention, but his eyes were closed as he spoke. "Son, this whole situation is a result of a very simple problem. Think on this so you will get the full understanding of what I'm saying. Take the word *truth*. In the Declaration of Independence it says, 'We hold these truths to be self-evident.' My interpretation is simply that the truth of God is man's evidence of his right to be free. If you don't believe in truth, you are enslaved. When Adam sinned, he declared his independence. Any person born after Adam is naturally independent from God and lives without the knowledge of truth. Until a person believes, he has no way of understanding truth. So when a declaration emphatically says that we hold these truths to be self-evident, unless a person understands what truth is, he can't receive freedom. God's own hand was right in the middle of the Declaration of Independence. He gave us His law for us to be successful and prosper. Like you just quoted from the Bible, it was also for us to follow.

"The modern progressive definition of the word *truth* is a completely different matter. What is meant by me saying modern probably goes all the way back to the end of the 1400s. Close to the same time the

Reformation was happening, so was the Enlightenment. Here two great powers were being established to gain control of the world. One force was a revival from God Himself that cost many reformers their lives. The other was a period of enlightenment during which man discovered his own definition of truth. Over many centuries this word was thought out and debated; lasting conclusions were made that set the stage for America today. Without God, man was left to his own devices, and without him even having an understanding, truth could not be understood. To sum up how independent man defines truth: truth is the conclusion or consensus of several groups with good intentions, to serve each other for the common good. This is what is now taught at all the colleges and universities as the real understood truth.

"You mentioned this before; past president Lyndon Johnson created a gigantic welfare state to help the down and out, the disenfranchised. By doing this he actually enslaved black America. His reason was to keep his party in power. For many years black America has voted for the Democratic Party, and will continue to do so. Many blacks fail to understand that the Democratic Party changed the economy so that the American workforce had fewer job opportunities. By federal design the job market dried up. The state then became a benevolent state and gladly provided for their daily sustenance. Welfare checks, food stamps, government housing, home loans, training programs, free medical care—as the list grew and continued to grow, the federal government went into great debt, without any intention of financial reconciliation. Some past presidents, such as President Obama, wouldn't even make a required federal budget, one that was required to be submitted to Congress.

"Remember John F. Kennedy's famous speech when he said, 'Ask not what your country can do for you, but what you can do for your country'? When a country or its people can't understand what truth is, then what LBJ did, and what Kennedy said, would be concocted truth that eventually enslaves.

"We weren't put here to serve America; we were put here to serve God in a free America. Jesse, we could be living in the last days, the very last of days. If this is so, then man, who chooses his own way, will have had his way and they still won't believe truth. You must always give them a choice. No matter what the consequences, all men must have a choice to follow truth. Actually we all do. It is always between God and each person; it always was and always will be."

It was late. Both dad and son sat quietly, silently prayed, and thought about what each had said that night.

Chapter 6

It's Never Too Late

Monday Morning, November 9, 2032

It was raining lightly, and snow was in the forecast. Governor Hall had left his Harley at the Alamo and was in the official governor's SUV, just outside Austin, making his usual morning phone calls. "Clint, I'm glad I caught you on the phone. Can we meet sometime this morning? I just heard on my radio that the Supreme Court will announce at ten in the morning eastern time their decision on giving Vernon Wiley a second term." Governor Jesse Hall was his normal excitable self as he spoke to Clint Ross, Texas's lieutenant governor.

"Yes," Clint said. "How about the Paris Coffee Shop right now? I haven't had any breakfast yet. I'll even buy."

"Great. See you there" was the governor's only remark before he hung up his cell phone. Out of habit the driver was already headed toward the Paris Coffee Shop, before the governor told him where he was going.

It was a very gloomy Monday morning. The progressives now totally ruled. Not by the time-tested edicts in the Constitution, but by fraud or misdirected truth. President Wiley continued to preach that the federal government's commonsense approach would eventually lead to a solution. He continually told the American citizens he would restore the middle class. The President said, "Everyone must come together to support the cause, he said; it is our only hope."

The electoral vote was very close, but President Vernon Wiley lost. He was counting on the Supreme Court to allow him a second term, the same way Al Gore tried previously, but this time the outcome would probably be different, because nine very liberal justices were sitting on the bench. If the present administration stayed in place, progressivism would continue to advance. The American public had been led to believe that their hope lay in Vernon Wiley and a common good for everyone. That is what most of the people believed. They had been told that although it would take a long time, they all had to sacrifice for the common good. The government had been saying the same story for decades. The rich had bled the nation to ruins, although the previously rich left America many years ago, along with the middle class. The new rich now came from government-mandated bureaucratic institutions like cap and trade. Every citizen was required to give their best for the good of all. They were told that if they did, the country would survive.

Hal Wilson, a moderate Republican, won the election to become the forty-eight president of the United States of America. During the campaign Hal spoke the truth. He told it like it was. He said what had to be done for America to regain herself. In essence he said that the American people had to be willing to provide for themselves and stop the government's programs, programs that drained the life from America. He said many times that although recovery would be painful, a drastic change was necessary. President Vernon Wiley had continued to blame everybody else for the country's woes. About half the people believed Hal Wilson and the other half believed Vernon Wiley. It was a divided America, with the people losing as usual. Dishonesty and deceit ruled the day.

In Texas, probably 80 percent of the people were opposed to the progressive party. Unemployment was around 28 percent and getting higher. Not much could be done to change the direction of America or of Texas. Unemployment everywhere else was about 35 percent. It had been years since anything had been paid on the national debt, the infrastructure was nonexistent, and the roads were unsafe, although not many people used the highways much anyway. The large trucks using the national highways were mostly federally owned and operated produce and cattle trucks. They carried foodstuffs from government farms to distribution and food-processing centers all across this once great land.

Somehow in all this mess almost everyone had been able to eat—not real well, but everyone had enough to get by. All these problems were systematically planned for only one purpose: to create a government of the party, by the party, and for the party. It worked; the progressives had convinced everyone that if they lost their power, there would be nothing: no food and no regulated electricity, and further cuts in medical care. As it stood now, the government was doing all it could to keep everybody fed. The public was told the job market would get much worse and that medical help for seniors would get even worse than it was already. The country believed that if the conservatives got in office, they might not have any health protection at all and many would starve to death. The ruling party convinced the masses that the situation was very bad, but could be getting much worse. It wasn't the party's fault. No one had claimed responsibility for this mass decades-old failure. The people followed like sheep and lived in fear of losing what little the state allowed each person to have.

Surprisingly, the sun started to appear as Governor Jesse's vehicle turned into the parking lot at the Paris Coffee Shop. He thought to himself, *This is Texas. How does this place stay open? There's never a crowd here anymore. The menu is very basic, and any corner that could be cut has been cut. Now you can get a table anytime of the day.* Almost out loud, he thought, *Somehow change must happen. We have to create change.* He could see Clint at the door, waiting for him. *This just may work. God help us—it just may work.*

Usually when two very good friends meet, they start talking and dispense with any formalities like shaking hands. As the governor saw his friend, Lieutenant Governor Ross, he automatically followed him to a more private corner seat. The coffee shop was a small place that they both frequented regularly. Somehow Clint usually arrived first and led Jesse to a corner where they could talk in private. The security detail could manage their duties of protecting the governor, and the small café could go on as usual.

As they slid into a booth, Jesse said, "What's on your mind, Clint?"

With a friendly yet somewhat sarcastic smile Clint replied, "You called me, Governor."

"Yes I did. My question to you is, what do we need to do to get well?" Governor Hall spoke with a very serious tone in his voice.

Just then a pretty waitress brought them bagels with cream cheese and coffee. Smiling, she said, "I guess you wanted your regular order, didn't you?"

Clint spoke up and said, "Yes, of course. That will be fine, Suzy. Just keep the coffee coming, please."

"What's your answer, Clint?" Jesse said, with obvious great interest.

Apparently Clint had spent some time thinking about a solution for America's decades-old decline and its turn to progressivism. He said, "I see only two alternatives: one is to secede from the union, and the other is to declare a strict adherence to the Declaration of Independence and follow the original US Constitution. These two documents have been cast aside, but today, realistically, they are our only hope. I believe that if we give Texans hope, they will follow, and then it will be a new day for America. For Texas to do either and have any kind of success we must debunk global warming. If we secede from the Union, it will be forced upon us. If we follow the Constitution, it will be forced on them.

"Hope must be accompanied by security. We must not ask anyone to sacrifice anymore unless the people will benefit instead of the state, but let's unite for real change—really believe in a different direction. The same direction our forefathers forged out of the wilderness and that made America great."

"Clint," Jesse said, "I just spent the weekend with my dad, and we talked about this very thing. It's the only way. We need to get Howard on board so we will all be in agreement. Today Vernon Wiley will more than likely win by Supreme Court decision. I don't think anyone will be surprised, and I don't think there will be much of a reaction. After the global warming summit decides in our favor, we must act fast. While the summit is taking place, we will have plans in place waiting for our okay to act.

"The first change in policy from the federal government mandates is to drill everywhere in Texas and in the Gulf waters. Open the refineries. But first we need to get Texas and most of the other states on our side. Many of the states have aligned themselves with the progressive movement. Perhaps the people in these states will influence a dramatic change in federal leadership."

Clint put his coffee cup down, and his eyes welled with tears. "Jesse, this has to work." Pausing to gain his composure and pointing toward heaven, Clint said, "Jesse, let's have a rally on the steps of the capitol building to announce the summit. We'll have the attorney general and several leaders of the legislature speak. I know a rousing black pastor who can help—even your dad; I remember listening to him. Let's get as much advance publicity as possible. If this could be carried nationwide, other states might join in.

"As soon as possible we'll call a special session of the Texas State Legislature and the cabinet. I think the first action is to recall the president, vice president, and Supreme Court. They have failed America and disregarded the Constitution. They're bound to obey our laws, but have failed in every way possible. You, Howard, and I could speak from your office and announce this action. Then in front of the world we'll call a special session to decide the proper response to President Wiley, Vice President Gerald Cunningham and all the Supreme Court justices."

Chapter 7

The Declaration of Texas

Monday, November 17, 2032

It was a chilly but sunny November afternoon, and the crowd was much larger than anticipated. Most of the national news outlets reported that at least a thousand angry people had congregated around Austin, and trouble was in the air. Actually the crowd was much larger; it was probably closer to fifteen thousand upset people looking for answers. The great crowd caused the news briefing to be moved outside the state capitol building. It delayed the start of the meeting from one o'clock to two.

The Texas Speaker of the House, Robert Bold approached the podium with his normal stoic persona. Slowly he looked over the crowd and said, "As a great state, we must speak truth to our citizens. You as citizens need to understand what truth is. We have only God, and God is all we need to change the wrong perpetrated by the evil men in office. The worst part is, we as a nation of free citizens allowed this to happen. What happened to America was one simple change. They gave one word its own meaning, and that changed everything.

"The public schools, colleges, and universities did their part. Churches became liberal and complacent and ended up being dark, empty buildings. There will always be two opposing parties, sometimes more than two, but the word *moderate* wooed the Republican opposition to progressivism many years ago. There aren't enough progressives to take over a nation or even the world, but they did. We were lulled into it. All they had to do was change the meaning of one word, the word *truth*. The great majority, the ones who vote in the middle, always win. These people stand for nothing. They aren't Democrats or Republicans, just people who are weak and can be swayed, people without truth. They are people without any concept of liberty and freedom at any cost."

Thousands of spectators had come to hear the speeches, although none of them knew what to expect. It was as if they needed to hear something to give them hope, and somehow those few words caused something unexpected to happen. At first a couple of people got on their knees as if to pray. In less than a minute, almost everyone was kneeling, hands lifted, and crying out to God. You could hear the people in unison pleading for God to help and crying out, "Forgive us, forgive us, God." Robert Bold, the Speaker of the House, then turned and extended his hand to Pastor E. G. Hill as if to guide him to the podium.

As Pastor Hill took his turn, he stood there unashamed, shaking his head and sobbing. He was visibly overcome by this unexpected turn of events. After some time the pastor regained composure and without saying a word started singing "I Surrender All." By now everyone was on their feet, arms lifted, and singing. When he finished the song, Pastor Hill stood still as if praying silently. After a brief moment he started praying aloud. "Dear Father God, You must be angry, very angry, with this generation and past generations, as You should be. Our hearts have gone astray, and we have not known Your ways. Father, have mercy on us and lead us back to You as a nation. Father, please forgive us, for You are the only way for peace and prosperity to again fill this great land. Amen."

Governor Hall came to speak as Pastor Hill sat down. No one introduced each other; it was about the message rather than about the person speaking. Jesse had prepared a speech, but the crowd changed that. Without hesitating, the governor said, "Today I have hope; I see that our only hope is in God. A long time ago things got turned around, and now everything is about serving a government. More than two hundred and fifty years ago, our forefathers started something: freedom from Great Britain and liberty for all Americans. The moment they declared independence, mighty forces came against them, visible forces from across the Atlantic Ocean. That was all we saw and who we fought. Our forefathers established a new country and fought mightily for this great new land. Other forces were already at work to create a government that we belonged to, not a government that belonged to us.

"We were blinded from the beginning. The only force we saw was what was visible. From Great Britain they came in many ships and great numbers, but with great sacrifice we finally won. As we grew, we had to be diligent against foreign powers with evil intentions. A great sacrifice has always been paid for this God-given freedom. Freedom has endured as an example of God's love toward us, and America has paid dearly for others to be free.

"Many great people sacrificed their lives for our freedom, and now America has chosen slavery. Again we must turn from slavery and be vigilant to stand for truth as people and as a nation. We must always be vigilant to expose those who desire their own concocted truth—a man-centered truth with only one purpose: to enslave everyone to a world system of government." Pausing and looking out over the crowd, Governor Hall said, "You bless me, and I love you all. This is a new day for Texas and America."

As the governor took his seat, Lieutenant Governor Clint Ross rose and took his place to speak. "I'm overwhelmed," he said. "President Wiley, with the help of the Supreme Court and past presidents, has stolen America. We let them do it, but no more; it is our America. After Japan attacked Pearl Harbor, Japan's Admiral Isoroku Yamamoto said to his staff that they may have awakened a sleeping giant. They did. Today I see hope in America. A giant has been awakened in America. You give us hope.

"As lieutenant governor of Texas, I come here today to tell all Texans, America lives. The executive branch and the legislative branch of Texas are united against the presidents treasonous acts. Howard Martin, our attorney general, will start the process of recalling all the Supreme Court justices and bring charges against Vernon Wiley. What Vernon

Wiley meant for evil is now turned in the opposite direction. It will be for good—I pray a lasting good. We owe thanks to Vernon Wiley for waking up America. If Vernon Wiley comes to Texas, he will be arrested and held on charges. If any Supreme Court justice of the United States comes to Texas, he or she will be held for legal determination. This is a new day for America." As Clint Ross turned and took his seat, he raised a clenched fist in the air, a symbol of victory. The crowd responded by doing the same as they cheered.

Attorney General Howard Martin was a short, quiet man who always considered each word carefully before speaking. He didn't mind pausing during a sentence to think through what he was about to say. He loved the written law and believed that each word from his mouth should be thoughtfully spoken. He did this to keep from offending the laws he loved and stood for. Many people didn't understand Howard. If he had been alive during the time of the writing of the Declaration of Independence and the Constitution, his name would have been etched in American history. As providence would have it, his name would be etched in history for the same causes as before, but 250 years later.

Now speaking, he started by saying, "We've all heard the saying that history repeats itself. Perhaps this is so. Perhaps we are destined to find out. It should be an odd statement to say this, but it is our only statement. All we have is God and what He gave us, the Declaration of Independence and the Constitution. That is all we need to restore Texas and America.

"Today unemployment in America is more than thirty-five percent. In Texas it's around twenty-seven percent. I really believe that when the economy gets so bad that all states have more than fifty-percent unemployment, the only jobs left will be government-supported work, and then gradually unemployment will slowly decrease. The reason is that finally, America will be no more. The economy will be irrelevant. People will be irrelevant. The state will reign supreme. By then God will be a long-forgotten myth. If we had stood before you ten years ago, would you have, could you have, surrendered to God and prayed like you just did? I don't know. What matters is what just happened. Now a deceived giant has awakened. We can't turn back.

"Little by little, word by word, truth was changed. Then all of a sudden we were killing Mother Earth and everyone was supposed to die. Nothing could be done except to bow down to whatever the Environmental Protection Agency declared. Nothing's ever been proven. The truth was distorted, and we were enslaved. Immediately Texas will start the legal process of prosecuting Vernon Wiley, and Texas will start legal action against the Supreme Court justices of the United States. They have broken the laws of our American Constitution. We are instructed in the Declaration of Independence what to do when a government assumes power over its citizens. Soon other states will join our great cause, and we will restore America.

"This movement against its citizens was started in earnest long before America was formed. It was defined during the Enlightenment period. A new order of understanding was created by man, but this new way of understanding excluded God. This all happened about the same time as the Reformation period. For the first time in history, the Bible was becoming accessible, and many men were martyred for God's truth. The world was changed in two ways. One way was slavery as ultimately set forth in the Enlightenment. The other way was that man could understand our God-given freedom through Jesus Christ. Both can't live in the same world in peace. Man as a whole failed to understand that all battles are spiritual. Man fought only through visible political means and lost. Jesus said, 'My kingdom is not of this world.' He rules through each person's heart, by each person's understanding what truth really is. Jesus also said, 'I am the way and the truth and the life. No man comes to the Father except through me.' Evil men can't understand these words, men who created their own definition of *truth.* Jesus also said, 'If you know the truth, then you will be set free.' Can we begin to understand these words? It is about understanding one or the other, plain and simple: one or the other.

"I would like to mention something of interest that propelled these two forces of vastly different realities to the front of many people's minds.

About 1440, the Gutenberg press was invented. For the first time in history man could communicate with the masses by the written word. As both the Reformation and the Enlightenment period were beginning to spread, the written word enabled almost everyone to discover their own meaning of truth. That was the start of mass media. It is no different today. We still have mass media, and there is still only one truth. Great scholars from great universities write theses on their definitions of truth. King Solomon once said, 'There is nothing new under the sun.' We still have mass media that promotes a world system, and our great universities are still defining their understanding of what truth is in their secular way of understanding.

"As we prosecute Vernon Wiley, Texas will form a legal scientific summit on global warming. All the rules for discovery will be honored. As this takes place, the findings will be disclosed and acted upon. Global warming is the driving force that ruined the world's economy. The economy was purposely ruined so a so-called benevolent country could come to the aid of its helpless citizens. If global warming can't be proved or if global warming is proved to be a hoax, then the state of Texas will act accordingly. The immediate national consequences will be that the government in place is suspect, as we all know very well. It will mean that Texas will serve only a newly, properly elected president. All EPA offices will be closed. We will confiscate all federal lands in Texas, as is our sovereign right. We will drill for oil and gas, and we will begin mining for rare metals, coal, and whatever we need to get people working for themselves instead of the state-operated systems. The automobile makers in Texas will begin making new cars—new cars with V8 engines in them, I hope. Maybe the churches will sing old gospel hymns, and rock and roll will come back. Is that too much to ask?

"If Texas stands alone, so be it: we will stand alone. We are called the Lone Star State, but I see hope again, as do my brothers and sisters standing with me. Men and women of Texas, you are family, and we have already won. Just by standing and choosing God and truth, we have won."

By now everyone was cheering, with tears running down their faces in emotional delight, something that had long been gone from every face in our great land.

Before Howard Martin could sit down, Pastor Hill stood beside him with his arm around his shoulder. Pastor Hill said in his loud, clear voice, "It feels great to be free. It feels great to be an American. God be with us again." Looking over the crowd, he said, "I will say to the world that all of these men have just spoken truth in such a way that no person should deny God's truth. Folks, many will still be deceived and continue to live accordingly. What I say to all people, to all people everywhere, is that we are free again. Let's set aside being a Democrat, let's set aside being a Republican. Together let's ask God what we should do, what He would have us do.

"Can anyone ever remember either party coming together for any length of time? No! They never do! Neither party can make good decisions, usually resulting in the moderates getting their way. These are people in the middle—people without true convictions, people who won't fight for what is right. People looking for truth but not knowing what truth really is—these are people who are held together by a godless, captivating philosophy, people who are dead to either side but remain slaves to their own false beliefs."

The pastor raised his hands and said, "Thank God, thank God," and then walked away.

Chapter 8

Expected Turn of Events, The White House

Wednesday Afternoon, November 17, 2032

Vernon Wiley, appointed leader of the United States of America, sat in the historic Oval Office in the White House and wondered what response would be most effective or whether he should respond at all. Texas had always gone against any efforts from Washington to unite the states with the federal government for the sake of progressivism. While he was in deep thought, his cell phone rang. It was the appointed vice president of the United States, Gerald Cunningham. Like most vice presidents Gerald was a figurehead. He attended funerals and spoke at insignificant government gatherings. His main function was a personal one for Vernon Wiley; he was a very good sounding board. "Hi, Gerald, I'm glad you called. Come over and let's talk. Uh, when can you come over? I guess you heard the latest news from Texas, didn't you?"

Gerald replied, "Yes, President Wiley, I will be there in about twenty-five minutes. And I did hear the speakers from the great state of Texas," he said, his tone disdainful.

Vernon Wiley continued to ponder the latest news developments from Texas as he waited for Gerald Cunningham to arrive. The favorable press did their part: as each speaker had their turn to speak, the TV screen showed only a small picture from a distance. The main picture on the TV showed the news commentator giving his take from his own view. It was very effective except for one conservative news outlet, the Eagle News and Broadcasting Company, or ENB. It was broadcast in its entirety. After the broadcast the conservative news commentators took calls from across America to get viewers' responses. This was done without any additional commentary influence.

Vernon Wiley sat at his desk with a cigar in his mouth. He had quit smoking cigars years earlier, but now he chews them and spits out the small pieces created from vigorous chewing. Mr. Wiley was a short, nearly bald man of sixty-plus years. His appearance was less than attractive, but when he spoke, one didn't remember his appearance. He had a way of captivating an audience, whether it was one person or a crowd. When he was on television, his aide always made certain the cameras maintained close-up shots at all times.

From the monitor on his desk Vernon could see Gerald down the hall from the Oval Office as he anxiously waited. He threw the wasted cigar in the wastebasket and went to the open door to receive him. Gerald loved coming to the White House. He had hopes of living here if Vernon ever vacated his office. It was looking doubtful. There were fresh flowers in a vase on Vernon's desk, and Gerald could smell both the fresh flowers and the wet cigar.

Without saying a word Vernon went to his desk and sat down. Vernon knew to be cautiously quiet and to let Gerald speak his mind first. He always did, and Vernon usually benefited from this approach. Vernon didn't say a word; he waited for Gerald to begin. This approach seemed odd but worked well for the many decisions that came from their cunning minds. Gerald sat down, clasped his hands behind his head, and slid himself comfortably into his seat. Nothing was said for five minutes or more. Finally Gerald spoke.

"Sir, there are two mighty forces at work here. Our side has always patiently waited for change, and change always favorably comes our way. We use the people to bring the necessary change to us. Over many years we changed how they view government. There are two powerful roots. One root is dying because the other root is killing it. It won't completely die, but it is helpless. This dying root will eventually render itself helpless. What I saw today was a surprise to everyone, including the speakers. The crowd knelt and prayed. They prayed to something they've long forgotten. If we give them enough time, they will forget and like dogs, return to their own vomit. That's their history."

Vernon said, "I understand that very well, Gerald, but what if the summit on global warming gives them a favorable ruling? What happens if they start drilling for oil and refining oil as before? If this happens, the unemployment in Texas will quickly be less than ten percent. If that happens, we're in trouble."

Gerald said, "Not necessarily. They may have a reprieve, but it will be short lived.

"The good old USA owes the World Bank more than three hundred trillion dollars. There is no such real entity as the World Bank, but the World Bank as it is known by everyone owns the world. There is only one healthy root. It is the World Bank; it's not us. It never was us. This will eventually cause the world to come under a unified government. Once this great but catastrophic event happens, there will be stability for all peoples, everywhere. I don't know how long it will take, but Texas can't stop it. They may slow it down, but it can't be stopped. We won't even have to fire a shot. We financially printed ourselves into submission for a much greater cause. The World Bank backed our dollars and everyone else's. It was so simple. The people had needs; we purchased their loyalty by creating a system where they needed us. They really have no choice. Man's personal liberty will give way for the betterment of all." Neither Vernon nor Gerald said another word; they just sat still, both of them smug, as if they had already won.

Gerald said, "Sir, you may consider this: Texas may eventually secede from the Union. That is their only realistic chance—a small one but a possibility. If they do, the result would be isolation from the world. Texas has enough resources to be an independent country on its own. They could have a stable economy, which would be meaningless in a world where an economy doesn't mean vitality anymore. If Texas prospers, we will have to isolate ourselves from them.

"Remember the Soviet Union? No one knew much about them until they joined the world community. They were isolated from us and us from them. In fact that may be our best response. We could go on the defense and say that we will always welcome Texas into the world community, but the requirement is the same for everyone: all must participate as world citizens of a unified community, united in caring for all. As we make our case to the world, we will separate ourselves from Texas but show the world that Texas is part of our family, and we're desirous of reunification."

The meeting was over, and Gerald was leaving the Oval Office when the phone rang. Vernon said, "Wait, Gerald. This is from the governor of Texas." Putting on the speakerphone, Vernon said, "Hello, Governor Hall. You've stirred up the whole country. Getting everyone riled up won't help Texas or America."

Governor Hall spoke up and said, "Vernon, I'm appealing to your common sense. Many states have voiced support for Texas and are looking forward to a ruling from the global warming summit. You already know the inevitable outcome, and it will destroy many of your party's schemes. My reason for calling is to ask you to correct this grave mistake. America should demand that you vacate the office of president. Also, America should determine the truth about global warming, not Texas, but we will prevail."

Vernon Wiley replied, "Sir, it's not my choice. I serve at the behest of the people's government. It is for the common good of all citizens, and you should understand that. Jesse, whatever the immediate outcome is, eventually we will win. That is what really matters—the final outcome. Jesse, thank you for calling, but my answer is no." Then Vernon hung up the phone, turned to Gerald, and said with a forced smile, "We may have to take two steps back."

That evening when the six o'clock news came on, many news pundits had all manner of explanations about what to expect from Texas. On some news outlets the commentator would be interrupted with an emergency warning and report that traveling in Texas might be hazardous at this time and that all citizens should exercise caution before entering the state. The ENB reported the conversation between President Wiley and the governor of Texas. Not much was said by the conservative news commentators. They listened to what the people had to say and let them speak their minds, and many did.

Chapter 9

Two Governments, One Country

Friday Morning, December 17, 2032

All the federal departments and agencies were in a state of confusion. Vernon Wiley expected this and hoped that by Inauguration Day on January 20, 2033, the country would be back to the new normal. His hopes were pinned on how the press supported him. No one knew ahead of time that Texas would turn everything upside down.

It appeared as if the intentions of Vernon Wiley and the party were well coordinated with the press, or most of the press. That wasn't the case at all. If the vice president or president or any leader from the progressive party made a speech, the progressive news system would carry that particular story until whatever desired effect was achieved. It was the cause that connected everyone, their own unified reality. What they said collectively became good and proper. What they said as truth would be truth by consensus. Very few people realized and understood that over many years the minds of the masses throughout the educated world were stolen. People who studied history and understood truth could see what was taking place. As Christianity was diluted, so were the minds of the masses. The people were unable to tell what was real and what wasn't. That is what man on earth wanted, and that is what they received. The evil intentions of their hearts became independent and separate from God, although many still prayed and went to church.

After the Supreme Court ruled against the proper and newly elected president, Hal Wilson, he withdrew to organize and assume his elected role as the president-elect in exile. He knew there could be dangers for his family; the vice president, Ginger Brown; and her family. No one knew his whereabouts, except for a few very trusted aides. Hal was a retired one-star general from the marines. He calmly made his assessment of the situation and acted decisively. Camp Pendleton, a sprawling marine base in California, would be his headquarters for the immediate future. Not many people knew of this particular place, but in a remote area of Camp Pendleton were more than adequate housing and office facilities. They had been built years ago but were seldom used. They had been created for foreign dignitaries or government officials who had to leave their countries and needed American protection; usually their home countries were American allies or served a purpose for America.

During this time of great turmoil, the Texas governor, lieutenant governor, and attorney general stayed in conference continually. Their choice meeting place was of course the Paris Coffee Shop. Until now, security hadn't been a factor, but Captain Ray Smith, being a cautious man, now thought otherwise. He didn't think anyone would shoot the governor, but a gas leak could occur, and the place where these men were could somehow blow up, thus ending their hope for Texas.

As Jesse, Clint, and Howard arrived, security was visibly intensified. Their regular visits were causing more of a crowd than previously. Captain Smith masterfully kept the press at a distance.

It was Friday morning, and Suzy had already brought their regular order for the governor and his close associates. Jesse said, "Howard, will you please bless the food so I can eat?" Smiling, Howard said his usual breakfast grace. As they ate, they each had a notepad on which they had listed topics to discuss. Jesse spoke up first. "Before this mess started, I had already planned to do the global warming summit. I'd already sent out e-mails and letters to numerous scientists to enlist their involvement and to get some sort of idea what we need to do. A few have replied, some saying it can be proved and most saying it can't be proved. Clint,

I've talked to a few of the legislators, and most of them were in favor of a summit. We normally will meet this January eleventh, but I think we need to have a special session just for this matter, probably around the first of December. Clint, you will need to get a special committee to oversee the committee. We may be rushing our summit agenda, but we need to get this resolved ASAP. Today I wanted to make a list of what we need to do and the order in which we need to do it. We need to try to stay ahead of Vernon Wiley and the party."

Clint spoke up. "I already have a list. Maybe Howard can tell us the feasibility of these different items."

Jesse said, "First, I have something more to say about the global warming summit. There is a meteorologist in Fort Worth I listen to sometimes. He had a special a few years ago about global warming. He is very smart, and I hope he will chair the summit. It would take away the political aspect. I think his name is Al Biggs."

Clint started speaking again. "First on my list is for Hal Wilson and Ginger Brown to run the exiled American government from Austin. I haven't contacted them, but I don't think they have any choice but to come to Texas.

"Number two is to ask the new dictator of America to relinquish all of the following documents: the Declaration of Independence, the Constitution, the Bill of Rights, and even the Gettysburg Address. These precious documents aren't of any value to the system of government in place at this present time. I know the federal government can't release them, but this may draw some people to our side. When we can, let's use the media for our benefit as much as possible. This is a great way to do just that.

"Number three is to confiscate all federal lands. This should be done as soon as we get a favorable ruling on global warming, but we should be prepared to move as soon as we receive the ruling. Since 2022 the federal government has controlled all our farmland and ranch land. Remember as the farmers' and ranchers' lands were being foreclosed on, the feds took control and let them work for the government. They had no choice. They control the meat processing plants and the transporting of all the products made and grown in Texas by Texans. We will help other states with our goods, but it will benefit Texas and the states with whom we have trade agreements. For too many years the feds have used food to control American citizens. We will go back to the old way, the way it was before—owned by citizens and sold for profit, thus creating jobs for many.

"If we secede the federal government will try to isolate us from the world and our fellow states. I hope in time the other states will join us. If they do, we will win sooner than later. If they don't, we will stand alone and win by ourselves. I guess this is why we are called the Lone Star State.

"The fourth item is somewhat risky, but we need to secure Texas. If we had marshal law, the federal government might be able to turn it against us. I think we need to have control of who belongs in Texas and who doesn't. If a person is not a citizen of the United States and living in Texas, they must leave the state. If they are Mexicans working here and have lived in Texas for a few years, they can get a temporary work permit. To do this they must register and pay taxes like everyone else. If a person is from another state and living with a Texas family, they must be registered. Other than that, this won't have any effect on the citizens of Texas. If an illegal alien or a noncitizen fails to register, they will be expelled immediately. The United States as it is now will come against everything we implement. This will make us safe and cause the other states to take notice of how it is supposed to really be for its citizens. This will also reduce unemployment considerably. If anyone is an undesirable, then we won't allow a permit. For years we have supported Mexico by having undocumented workers siphon money from us to them. No more.

"I know you've already thought about some of the things I just mentioned—we discussed some of them before—but this may be the most important one of all. Immediately, like right now, we need to have our own currency. The Constitution allows a state to have its own currency only if their standard is gold or silver. When America was in its infancy, cash flow and monetary resources were nonexistent. The newly formed federal government was very limited because it lacked revenue and didn't have enough resources for what was needed to operate properly.

"Let's form a new banking system, an independent Texas banking system. We will print silver and gold certificates that will be backed dollar for dollar by gold or silver. The standard will always be gold or silver. This will always keep Texas from going into debt. Although the newly formed illegal federal government has voided all rules and regulations, whatever laws we have will be observed."

Before Clint could continue, Howard said, "Hey, buddy, how are you going to get enough gold and silver to run the newly formed United States?"

Clint said, "I think this will work. We will have a new and separate IRS in place of what we have now. Our tax rate will favor business and will not be burdensome to the citizen. We will set an example for America. This will take time but will not alleviate a great need for funds to operate on. To jump-start the New America we will ask every Texan to sell their gold and silver to the New America. In return they will have appropriate shares of the confiscated ranches and farmland. The federal lands where oil, gas, and rare metals are waiting to be mined and drilled will be turned back to the citizens. This should finance the New American banking system. It should also allow all Texans to participate in their country. The banking system will own the acquired gold and silver and lend money to the banks and different businesses. Instead of taxing the banks we will make a profit the same as they do by lending them money. This should quickly give us a robust economy.

"As we enact different measures to establish our states' rights, it will appear as if we are seceding from the Union. Eventually we may have no choice but to secede. In the interim I think we should call our effort the New America. It won't be a declaration of secession, but it will put the country on notice and may wake up some of the other states.

"A potential problem is that if any other state wants to unite with New America, they will have to create their own economy. This will maintain a weak federal government, as it should have been from the beginning. I hope if all states reunite, we can maintain our sovereignty, which is our strength.

"As a backup plan we should encourage all ranchers and farmers to plant crops and raise as much cattle and food as possible. All power plants should operate at a hundred percent as soon as possible. Let's stop any restrictions on electricity." Clint then said that that should about cover everything.

Howard spoke up and said, "In Texas we have more bases and military installations than anywhere else in the country. If we have to, we can recall all military personnel from the services and take control of our bases. We may need to get advice from active military leaders to see where they stand. Also, we should be very careful and not create the impression that we wish to start a civil war with America, but if we control most of the military, we will have a great advantage. This is a delicate matter that we should approach very carefully, but we must approach it nevertheless.

"Vernon Wiley will say we should all work for unity and reconciliation for the good of all. As these developments take place, our public stance will be to unite America with its proper elected president and let it be known that our sole purpose is to restore America to what it was before progressives took charge."

Governor Hall spoke up. "Howard, I think you and Captain Smith should take an Air National Guard plane as soon as possible to visit the president. Whatever he decides to do—stay in California or come to Texas—we need to have strong lines of communication with him. He needs to know we will not turn back and that we will support him in any way possible."

Chapter 10

Howard Martin Meets President Wilson

Saturday, December 4, 2032

Thomas Hardy, the leader of the famous Texas Rangers, and Captain Ray Smith quietly united to contact and set up a secret meeting with President Wilson and Texas Attorney General Howard Martin. Not much was told to Howard Martin about the trip. The purpose was to communicate Texas's support and offer a safe place to run an exiled country. No one knew if the real president was in danger, or if political or physical harm could come from this trip if the press or Vernon Wiley knew about it beforehand.

It was late Saturday night, about the time Howard and Wilma usually went to bed, when the doorbell rang unexpectedly. Howard knew who it probably was. Looking at his wife, he said, "Honey, remember the other day I told you I would be leaving on a secret trip? Well, it's time."

Wilma, looking worried, said, "Will you be safe? When will you be back? You can answer that, can't you?"

Howard held her close and said, "I should be back late Monday, and there's no danger involved in this trip." Howard had a bag packed near the door and hadn't yet changed into his pajamas he could leave immediately with Captain Smith, who was waiting at the door.

It was dark, and Howard didn't recognize the car waiting in the driveway. It was a personal car. Howard thought that was odd but kept his thoughts to himself. As he neared the car, he could see Thomas

Hardy at the wheel. *This must be Thomas Hardy's personal car,* he thought as he opened the car door. As the three drove away, Thomas said, "Sir, we're going to fly out of Camp Mabry, but we need to stop by my house and change vehicles. I live on the way."

Captain Smith was sitting in the front passenger seat and remained serious and silent. Howard was sitting in the backseat by himself. Although he was slightly amused, he thought it wise to put on a serious front. "Yes, sir, that will work for me," Howard replied somewhat awkwardly. As Thomas Hardy's car approached his house, the garage door opened to reveal a military vehicle parked inside with a driver waiting to embark again.

As they drove toward Camp Mabry, Captain Smith turned toward Howard and said, "Sir, as we drive onto the base, it will appear normal to be in a military vehicle. We will be waved through the front security gate and directly onto the waiting plane. If we were in a private car, we could be detained, and it could cause a problem."

"Yes, sir. I do understand, and I very much appreciate the care given to secrecy."

The plane waiting for Howard and his party was a small military jet, something a four-star general would use. The plane's engines were already running, and they were cleared for takeoff. Once in the air Captain Smith would have time to brief Howard on the schedule and plans already made for him with President Wilson.

Howard was told that the trip would take about three and a half hours, but because they were crossing time zones, they would lose only an hour. Captain Smith went on to tell Howard that the meeting would be the next day at ten in the morning California time. They would spend the night on base and return Sunday after the meeting.

After arriving and having dinner, Howard called Wilma to let her know he was all right and when to expect him back home. His accommodations were adequate; he had a large bed, a chair, and a dinner table with its own chair. He put his suitcase on the table and opened it and thought to himself, *This will do fine for the time I'm here.* From his room he could hear seagulls squawking. He decided to go outside for a breath of fresh air. The moon lit the sky, and the seagulls were visible and noisy. Howard could hear the waves rolling on the beach in the distance. It was a peaceful night.

Morning came fast, and Howard didn't have a discussion planned for his time with the new forty-eight president of the United States. He thought he would see how it went and respond accordingly. They arrived at President Wilson's house with a small military escort. It was a large house, and a few cars were there already. Howard didn't know what to expect but thought, *My mission is one of support, and that is what I will offer.* As they walked from the car to the front door, Howard thought his traveling companions were a little edgy. *Perhaps it's part of their job to be on guard at all times.* Before Captain Smith could ring the doorbell, President Wilson opened the door. There was no security in the house; just a few people were there, including Ginger Brown, the vice president. Both President Wilson and Vice President Brown greeted Howard and the men accompanying him very warmly.

After everyone was properly introduced, President Wilson said, "Let's go to the den for our visit. Before we start, does anyone want coffee or water?"

Everyone responded the same: "No thanks, I'm fine."

President Wilson then said, "My next question is, is this meeting concerning any national security matter?"

Howard replied, "No, sir, I don't think so."

The president said pleasantly, "We are making progress. Mr. Attorney General, would you like a private meeting or can we get started with everyone who is already present?"

Howard said, "Mr. President, we can all attend this meeting as far as I'm concerned." By now everyone was either seated or in the process of sitting down as Howard continued to speak. "President Wilson, Vice President Brown, the state of Texas has sent me to offer support. Also, Mr. President, we would offer accommodations in Texas for you and your staff. I really don't have any more to add except to let you know that I, along with Governor Hall, Lieutenant Governor Clint Ross, and most of the legislators, support your administration, and we jointly offer

Texas and its resources. Texas governor Jesse Hall wanted me to come to California to personally start a dialogue with your administration. We don't know what response Vernon Wiley will have toward you or toward Texas. We do know that somehow the people of Texas have expressed a growing dislike for a progressive, totalitarian America." Smiling, Howard looked directly at President Wilson and said, "What say you, Mr. President?"

President Wilson paused momentarily before speaking. "First I want to thank you for the kind offer you just made. The last few days have been agonizing for myself and Vice President Brown; my days are spent reading and trying to get some kind of insight so we can determine what to do next, and I'm very glad you're here to offer support. I'll try to express my feelings and concerns. Last month when the leaders from Texas and the pastor spoke, it seemed to me that the crowd was having some kind of religious experience. I'm not sure what that really means. I'm not a religious person, and their response was unusual. I don't know what to think about such a response.

"This is what I keep going over and over in my mind. In the last few days I've read the Declaration of Independence, the Constitution of the United States, the Bill of Rights, and the Gettysburg Address, plus old magazines and many famous speeches. Let's take the Declaration of Independence. This was a process. It didn't happen overnight. There were many great discussions and passionate debates before America went forward with its independence. When the American Revolution started, the people weren't prepared, but they were ready to die for an infant America. The Civil War was about a cause both sides would have died for. Just think: it's been almost a hundred years since World War Two, the last war America won. America is only as great as her people. America died a long time ago. If the people wanted freedom, America would already be free.

"I believe at this time that our best option is to stay here in California and see how things develop. Later we may need to move to Texas. I support everything that is being done in Texas. This may be the start of a new America or it may be the final nail in her coffin."

As President Wilson finished his brief but compelling speech, Howard had mixed thoughts. He was surprised that President Wilson wasn't a man of faith. He had assumed he was. He wondered how many great men had led America without faith in God as a foundation for everything they did. Was Texas experiencing something that was exclusive to Texas? Howard asked the president, "Sir, have you received support from any governors or congressmen?"

President Wilson replied with a somewhat sad look on his face, "No, not really. I've had many conversations, but most were with politicians positioning themselves for their personal benefit. In other words, they will go wherever the wind blows them. The same sickness most citizens have is the same sickness everywhere."

Howard thoughtfully said, "I see. It's very hard for me to understand, but I do see."

Ginger Brown was a beautiful redheaded woman in her fifties. She could be quiet for a while, but sooner or later she spoke her mind. She said, "Gentlemen, I'm sorry; usually the vice president just listens, but I do have something I wish to add to this discussion."

Before she could continue, the president smiled and said, "Ginger, this is the very reason I wanted you to be my vice president. Speak your mind, please."

Everyone smiled as Ginger Brown spoke. "This has been on my mind for several days, and now is a good time to speak my mind. I'm not a very religious person either, but what if God is doing something special? I think we need to be attentive. I don't know how to determine whether it is God or perhaps the people being unified for a noble cause. I'm sure there are many who do believe; maybe they are praying and their prayers are being answered. There are no laws against believing in God, but at the same time, if God can motivate the people and change America, then I say more power to Him." She smiled, and added, "Or Her."

As Ginger Brown finished speaking and returned to her normal quietness, the president added, "This is another great difference between the Republicans and the Democrats: we do believe in freedom of religion."

Howard thought to himself, *This is how America arrived at where it is today. Everyone can worship God, but most don't.*

No one person needed to say the meeting was over. Everyone had a chance to speak, and some did. It was important that Texas understand its position with the government in exile and what it needed to do. It took only a few minutes for each person to speak his or her mind, and that was about it. As everyone said their good-byes and went toward the waiting vehicle, Captain Smith excused himself and spoke privately with President Wilson, and then joined the others. No one spoke; it was a short and quiet ride to the waiting plane. Once in the plane, Captain Smith shared with everyone that he had told the president that there was a lot of uncertainty and that no one knew what was in the future for America or Texas. "I suggested a liaison between him and the Texas leadership, a method by which either he or our governor can maintain communications to maximize our support and security. I'm sorry I didn't mention it beforehand; I thought one of you would bring it up during the meeting. The meeting was over and I acted on my own. I hope I didn't speak out of turn."

Howard spoke up and said, "Captain Smith, we were all in an awkward position, and none of us knew exactly what we were going to say. We mostly wanted to offer support. I'm glad you had the foresight to do what you did. It needed to be said, and thanks for speaking up."

The trip home was uneventful; Howard was quiet and had a lot on his mind.

Chapter 11

The New America

Monday, December 6, 2032

Governor Hall sat in his office, impatiently waiting for Clint and Howard to arrive. The governor had so many things on his mind, he didn't know how to begin. Usually when one person shared his thoughts, the other two had the same general mind-set. Governor Hall wondered to himself how many people in America were thinking the same way he was. About the very time that Jesse was going from sitting in his chair at his desk to looking out his window, Ruby, his secretary, called him on the intercom. "Governor, your party has arrived. I will send them in. Would you like coffee or anything to eat?"

"Yes, we would like coffee, and I'll ask if they're hungry. Thanks, Ruby." After his reply the governor sat back in his chair.

The door to the governor's office was usually propped open. As Howard and Clint entered the large room, they both went to the chairs they usually sat in when visiting Governor Hall. Jesse arrived at the large door as both men entered. He leaned halfway into the hall to tell Ruby the door would be closed but to come on in when their coffee was ready. As everyone got comfortable, it was obvious that everyone had something very important to say.

Jesse spoke up first and said, "First I think we need to hear about Howard's weekend trip to see President Wilson."

With a humorous smirk Howard said, "I agree," and then spoke seriously. "The meeting was very brief and very interesting. I shared that Texas would offer sanctuary to him and his staff if needed, as well as any other support he might need in the future. He said two things that caused me to think about what we are doing in Texas. The first interesting statement he said was that if the people in America wanted freedom, they would already be free. He wants to see what America really wants before he acts. The other was that he isn't a man of faith. Ginger Brown said the same thing. I must be naïve, because I assumed most people believe. I guess if they did, everyone would know about their faith and we probably wouldn't be going through what we're going through.

"We met for an hour or less. There wasn't much to be said. It was an odd meeting. As we left, Captain Smith met with President Wilson and suggested we maintain a good line of communication. I was glad he thought of that before we left. As we move forward with whatever plans we have, we need to be very mindful of the people. Do they want freedom, and will they be willing to pay whatever is required for it?"

Both Jesse and Clint knew Howard was finished speaking about his trip. Jesse spoke first and said, "Very interesting, Howard. What you just said is very interesting. Clint, what are your thoughts? What's next for the people of Texas?"

Clint started by saying, "So far we've had a rally. It was very good, and it motivated us to think about liberty for the people of Texas. I must say that what Howard said about President Wilson made me think hard. I've already had many thoughts about which direction to take and how to set this great plan of liberty in motion. Remember when former president Wiley said he served at the behest of the American people? That is his understanding of what is true. It could very well be that is the same understanding the American citizens have. If we have many grand plans and schemes for a New America but don't have a people who are hungry for true change and a new way of life, then we're wasting our time. We're sunk before we get started. We're dead in the water.

"These are some of my thoughts. We know very well that most of the large newspapers agree with the status quo, even in Texas. The newspapers say what we say from their perspective. In every city—even in the small cities—there is a newspaper. Usually it is used for advertising and a way to pass out coupons. Let's each of us send articles that clearly express our beliefs and our plans. Let's tell everyone how America is supposed to be. At the same time we should share with Texans that we have turned away from God and that as we reclaim America, we want to search out God and include Him in our lives. We should get as many like-minded people involved in writing these articles as possible. This should be a very grassroots plan that will energize a base of an excited New America.

"At the same time we must have the support of the state legislators. We need to have a meeting with Robert Bold, the Speaker of the Texas House. I'm sure he will support us, but if we leave him out, it could be problematic. Soon I hope we can form committees on many of the issues we need to address. As we move along, we should pass along to Texas what we're doing. This should be done through the small newspapers throughout Texas. I truly believe that if we have all of Texas with us, we can't fail. If we don't, we will fail before we start. Some of the committees will need to be closed and secret. If Vernon Wiley learns of our ambitions before we have the people behind us, he could rush in troops and declare martial law. If he did such an act, I think it would ultimately backfire and perhaps cause other states to join us. Vernon thinks from the depths of his dark heart that the forces are with him, whatever forces he may believe in. He thinks that no matter what happens, eventually he will win and his cause will reign supreme through his view of America and his new world system.

"I pray to God that He is on our side. The Old Testament speaks of God letting His people be taken into captivity because of their disobedience. We are no different. He also showed mercy after captivity. This is good, because America is being held in slavery to this ungodly system and our unbelief as a nation. History is always a rerun of what's happened before. Wouldn't you think we would learn our lesson? I'm going to pass out an outline of what I think we need to do. We can have further discussion on each topic and how to proceed.

"As I just mentioned about writing articles for the small newspapers throughout Texas, this should be done with the intention of uniting everyone for liberty. At the same time it can't be a long process. As soon as we have a great majority of this state behind us, we should act fast and separate ourselves from the federal government. I'm not sure how to proceed with such an endeavor. I would think it would be immediate. In our meetings we've hinted at secession. My thoughts are that the federal government has separated itself from the original American constitutional system and we are declaring America as our way of life as it was once before and as it should be.

"For reasons I can't fully grasp, the progressives present themselves as victims and on the side of a perceived righteousness. They go against God and His word but convince the masses their way is for the common good and must be followed. This causes our side to naturally appear as the usual bad guys. They have denied God and cast Him from America, but somehow they project themselves as hope. It doesn't even matter how bad it is and how they have constantly screwed up. Most citizens have been deceived and are delusional in their thinking, but at the same time they support the 'common good' mind-set. They have been duped into believing we must all suffer for mankind. If we give most of what we have to the federal government, we will ultimately be better off and will have done the right thing for the "new world order."

"One more thing as I pass out my 'manifesto of liberty.' Perhaps we should have a very secret meeting with the military leaders, the legislative leaders, and the members of the Texas Supreme Court. At this meeting we will go for broke. If these leaders support us, then our next step should be separation from the federal government. We will need to communicate a plan of separation. By now I'm sure these leaders are expecting something like this from us. Whatever we do, or however we do it, a small few must be in control until we have stability. These three groups must be involved but be willing to let a small body of leaders guide Texas through this period. This manifesto must be the articles that govern the new government. Ideally what we should do is have the governor as acting president, with the chief justice of the

Supreme Court and the most senior leader of the Texas National Guard sharing in guiding Texas through these times. All the other branches of state government will be informed and kept abreast of the changes and actions of the new president of the New America. The president will solely have the singular right to make decisions. The newly appointed chief justice and the secretary of defense will assist but not have the final say in all matters. All government bodies will meet and carry on as usual but won't have any power to change whatever the new president decides.

"Once the new country is stabilized, the Constitution will be in effect. As we gain strength and security, different agencies will be able to operate as they should under a constitutional government.

"There are a few items I would like to include in the Constitution. The first is that we are a Christian nation, and we honor and serve God as a nation. We owe Him our all, and recognize Him as the only and true God. To be a citizen in good standing, faith in God is not a requirement, but as a nation we owe Him our allegiance. This statement will be the first declaration in the new Constitution. Psalm 33:12, 'Blessed is the nation whose God is the Lord,' will be our national verse and prayer. When the Constitution was written, the argument for secularism started, and eventually it won. I would also include in the new articles of government that this article can't be amended.

"Another item is that the president can't use executive privilege or mandates to govern. The Constitution and the laws passed by Congress will serve the government well in all matters. All agencies will be regulated by Congress and will not be able to regulate themselves.

"It the president disregards the laws of the nation, Congress can independently bring him to proper justice. Men, we can adjourn for a while and read the handouts."

Jesse spoke up and said, "I think we need to read again what Clint has prepared, then we need to respond. It's time to act. As he spoke, I thought about who would be best as president. I believe any one of us could be the first president of New America. As governor I would qualify, but I see that either of you would be just as qualified. Today let's discuss who should be the new president. Whoever we decide on, I would hope that we remain together for support and leadership." Looking at his watch Jesse said, "I'm hungry. It's eleven thirty. Let's eat. I'll get Ruby to order some food for us; I'm surprised she hasn't asked us what we would like for lunch. How does a sandwich with a salad sound?"

Clint and Howard said at the same time, "I'm hungry—anything will do." Clint said, "One more thing: I wrote this from my heart, so it will need to be formally rewritten and edited."

Chapter 12

Time to Cut Bait

2:30 p.m., Monday, December 6, 2032

By now it was obvious that all three men had a grievous task ahead of them. Until then, ideas had been shared and hope for the future was just an idea being talked about. Perhaps it was a concern, knowing that whatever happened would come from these men. It seemed as if it had been a long time since everyone had eaten their lunch and finished reading the papers provided by Clint. Jesse wanted to speak but felt like all three men were in deep thought about what they had just read. Jesse spoke after a period of brief silence. "Today may be the beginning of the real New America. I'm not sure but my gut feeling is that we need to respond as quickly as possible. A saying fishermen often say is that it's time to cut bait. Once you cut the bait, you must go fishing. Men, it's time to cut bait.

"Yesterday I had coffee with an old friend from Fort Worth. When I attended college at Texas Christian University years ago, I worked for Jim in the summer doing construction work. We've stayed in contact over the years and have coffee every now and then. I asked Jim how his family was and found out his mother had passed on. He told me something that has been on my mind since yesterday. Some time back, his mother had a stroke. He knew she wouldn't be able to return home. Jim has five sisters; he knew if he met with his sisters to discuss their mom's future in a nursing home, the meeting would end up in family chaos. Nothing would be solved, and their mom would return home, with each daughter trying to care for her. Without telling anyone, Jim made plans for his mom to go from the hospital to a nursing home. He gathered the sisters together the day before and told them of his decision. They all cried but were very relieved. This could have backfired, but Jim made the right decision. Guys, we have to act, not legislate.

"There are a lot of issues we need to be on top of. To secede from the national government, we need to have one interim leader. He needs to be able to control the economy and the military, provide food and safety, and organize a new country."

Howard said, "The governor of Texas is the commander in chief of all the military branches of service in Texas. We all know this, but we could select one high-ranking leader to be the secretary of defense, in charge of all military operations. This could consolidate our power.

"Another important issue is operating money. When we go to our own money system, we will need to have enough resources to fund the new federal government and the military, and provide the necessary services a country needs to provide. These issues may not be solvable problems, but we won't know until we actually break from the national government. How do we operate until we acquire all the gold and silver in Texas? I wish there were some way we could obtain gold and silver from the federal government before we acted. No one knows how much gold and silver the financial institutions in Texas have on hand.

"Wage and price controls: we must set limits on just about everything until the economy has a life of its own. We must be quick and decisive on all matters. Although one person should be in charge, I can see that the new president of a new country must be well prepared and act decisively."

"Men," Jesse said as Howard stopped talking and looked somewhat weary. "Last month Becky brought her grandmother to live with us through New Year's. I've been so busy, I haven't had time to be a husband, dad, son-in-law, son, or maybe even a good governor. Let's all pray and think through what we should do for the next few days. We will divide up some tasks that will help us act when it's time. If we can possibly get prepared, I would like to act on the first thing after the New Year. Mr. Wiley will be sworn in as our illegitimate president on the twentieth. We can't stop that anyway. Then let's come together next year on Monday, January 3, 2033. Gosh, that sounds funny. It seems as if 2013 was just yesterday. I don't think we could have a special session this month. But the next few days will give us time to organize and talk to a few key people.

"Clint, you do whatever research you can on making money—legal gold and silver certificates. Find out how long it will take to go from design to print and distribute. Also somehow get an estimate on the amount of gold and silver in Texas. Find out how quickly we can gather gold and silver and start a banking system with our own separate monetary system, and how and where we should keep our gold and silver. And try to spend as much time with your family as possible." Jesse smiled as he made his last statement. "No one needs to be told about the secrecy of what we're doing. Some leaks may occur, but let's be as careful as possible.

"Howard, find out who should be secretary of defense. You might even visit with him if you think it could help. I wouldn't tell him too much, but you can try to understand how he feels about what is happening to America. Also find out about the commanders of the military installations in Texas, if they are from Texas. Find out about the coast guard and navy bases. If you can, find out how many people are serving in the American military services, and how many are from Texas. Also don't forget to spend time with Wilma this Christmas."

Then with a wily smile on his face, Jesse said, "After we get back from Hawaii." He laughed at his joke. Clint and Howard didn't laugh. "Okay, not so funny. What I will do is see what is involved in securing our borders and the Gulf Coast. I will try to get as much information as possible on wage and price controls. We will somehow need to distribute food and keep everything running. When the federal government's money stops, we must intervene with our own. Social Security payments, the hospitals, and the utility companies must keep on running. If we don't make a good transition, we could have panic and chaos. If that happens, the federal government could keep the panic alive and we could lose before we get started."

Before the men left, they all stood up, held hands, and prayed. Afterward, Clint said, "Men, let's cut bait."

Chapter 13

Equality for Everyone

December 17, 2032

As darkness oozed from the depths of hell and its shadow covered the earth, almost everyone was blinded from understanding truth. They were unable to see what was in store for humanity. This day was formulated during the Enlightment by men who created their own truth, but was enabled at the time Adam ate the forbidden fruit.

President Wiley waited eagerly for his yearly holiday party guests to arrive at the White House. This year he had invited the rulers of several foreign countries: Russia, China, Japan, India, Germany, England, and France. Of all these countries France was the least, in size and might, but somehow France had political power and influence that would be used without hesitation if needed. At this time in history the ambitious US president did not want any problems from France.

President Wiley was accompanied as usual by the vice president, his most trusted adviser. The informal gathering would start at six o'clock with dinner. After dinner both President Wiley and Vice President Gerald Cunningham would meet separately with each head of state. The French president would probably be the second or third to meet with Wiley.

As it stood now, the G22 world leaders controlled the world's economy. The best estimate was that the participating countries controlled nearly 88 percent of the gross world production. The problem was that their control was indirect. The IMF, or International Monetary Fund, appeared to be a neutral world body. The truth was that almost all nations were controlled to various degrees by these two groups. The different world leaders had tentatively agreed to a more direct and acknowledged "one-world government." Each country had expressed a dedication to world progressivism, but hesitated because of a concern about citizens' reactions once these plans were implemented.

Most citizens throughout the world didn't fully understand their nations being controlled by a one-world body. For the last thirty or forty years the United Nations and world leaders with a worldview had directed their nations to a one-world community. The G8 Summit, the G20 Summit, and now the G22 Conference had evolved to a point that they were the real puppet masters. If one major country, a country like the United States, remained independent and maintained a strong military force, it would be a threat to the new world order.

The leaders in attendance at the party were curious about how all of the states, except Texas, had failed to challenge President Wiley on stealing the presidency; that was the purpose of this meeting. President Wiley intended to convince each world leader that shortly after January 20, he would be turning the United States over to a one-world body—that is, if everyone else did too.

The president and vice president greeted each dignitary as they arrived. A small band played soft music in the corner of the White House state dining room. By six fifteen everyone was seated and dinner was about to be served. A few of the world leaders had their translators with them, but almost everyone understood and spoke English. President Wiley whispered privately in the ear of Vice President Gerald Cunningham that he had decided to speak to everyone at the same time, and then answer questions after his speech. After hearing this, Gerald whispered to the president, "Sir, this is well and good, but it may cause a security problem. If someone leaks this, it could be disastrous to our plans." President Wiley was walking toward the band with the vice president at his side. He wanted to formally greet the guests, but first he responded to Gerald, "Yes, you are correct, but any person here could do the same for political leverage, if they wanted."

As the president took the microphone, he announced that he and Gerald Cunningham would be available to answer any questions and drinks would be served. The White House security was told to keep everyone off the premises; the president didn't want a reporter snooping around during this special event. Or anyone hearing what would be said at this very secret meeting.

President Wiley smiled and nodded at the seven smiling people who stood behind him with microphones. Each person held a flag extended on a pole with the symbol of the new world order on the flag. "My friends, you are welcome in this place. It is a great pleasure and honor to be with dear friends from different parts of the world. I hope we can grow in our trust for a common cause, to serve all humankind throughout this planet. Let us share a minute of silence for reflection and prayer." Some of the leaders prayed, but most simply observed silence. As this minute was taking place, the seven smiling people on the stage went to each table. When the minute expired, the band started playing. It was a very popular song from the seventies by John Lennon's, "Imagine." Each singer sang the song in the native tongue of the dignitary sitting at the table.

The song was about imagining a place and time with no God and no hell, with everybody living in peace. As the singers finished the song and left the room, there was applause. The people in attendance seemed to enjoy the selection.

Dinner was served, and everyone was made comfortable. After dinner drinks and coffee was offered and served. The room was emptied except for the president, vice president and guest. The president took the microphone, and said, "World leaders, for more than two hundred years Europe and America have had a democratic form of Government," "During this time many became rich. While the rich got wealthier, many became poorer. This was not an equitable way for people to treat each other.

"Without equality for everyone, man will be at his worst. During the same time the world had countries under communist rule. It was worse because no one kept the communist leaders in check. The time is now for each country to surrender itself for the common good. I've dedicated my life to world equality, and now it is within reach.

"This is the plan. It is basically what each of us has talked about in the past, but now it is time to implement it. Once we unite, most nations will join us. The first and most immediate thing to do is for all countries to turn over their military to the United Nations. In America the president's greatest responsibility is to defend and protect the country. This, then, will be the responsibility of the United Nations. Once America's vast military complex is surrendered for the common good of world peace, America will not have the ability to defend itself anymore. I believe that once all the world's military might is controlled only by the United Nations, then as a world body we can eventually reduce the world's armed forces.

"We know most of the Muslim nations and Israel will remain separate. We will need to maintain a military strong enough to defend ourselves against military aggression and terrorist attack. Imagine—can you imagine how the world will prosper once we establish world peace? I once read somewhere, 'They will beat their swords into plowshares and their spears into pruning hooks. Nation will not take up sword against nation, nor will they train for war anymore.'

"This tremendous resource then can be used for the betterment of the people of the world.

"All debt will be canceled, and every country will be even. We will have one currency for everyone, and there will be no borders, because there will be no enemy with evil intent. We heard the song 'Imagine,' but let's not just imagine; let us all unite as one.

"As it stands now, every country is in a deep depression. Unemployment is very high, and people are going hungry. Our number-one goal and duty is to provide food and medical care for everyone. Every country will still have a government. Now the new duties of each country will be to do its part to feed its own and its neighbor. This will be done through the new world order. Everyone will have the same as everyone else, according to size, and as soon as we all unite in one accord, we will overcome the mistakes of the past."

By now everyone was standing and clapping their hands. President Wiley was having the best day of his life.

Because of the applause the president stopped speaking. He thought it best to take questions. Instead of asking if anyone had a question, he remained silent. Everybody had questions. The president said, "It's early, and before we part, all questions will be answered as best I can." President Benoit Marcel from France stood up without being acknowledged; he seemed the most eager to speak. He stood up and asked sarcastically who would be the new "king of the world." The president smiled and replied, "I would love to be, and so would you. We will all have our turn to be world president. In the G22 Conference there are six groups of nations, with seven countries in each group. The new world president will be from a different country every two years. Eventually everyone will be the king of the world." This brought laughter from everyone. He continued, "Before being the president you must be vice president, so the president and vice president can work together. The same method will be used for the World Bank and the United Nations. We will truly have one currency for every country, and all countries will be the same."

The president of Russia stood up and raised his hand. With a strong accent he said, "Mr. President, this will be very hard to implement. What are your plans to do this great new thing for the world? How can we change from where we are now to where we need to be?"

President Wiley was pleased to hear these remarks from President Oner. "Sir, sometime in February all involved countries should meet. We will meet to enact emergency measures to deal with the world's worsening problems. We will stay in conference until everything is resolved. Then each country will be allotted a certain time to respond to their new duties. We all have to agree. If for some reason we can't come to an agreement, then this opportunity may fail. If that happens, many countries will fail. This is the only way."

It looked as if all the questions that needed to be answered had been answered at this time. A few of the world leaders were mingling, but most had left. President Oner approached President Wiley and hugged him. "You are great. This is a great day for Mother Earth. Long live President Wiley," and he lifted a glass to him in honor.

President Wiley responded by saying, "You are kind to say those words. This is a time in history when we can all rule together in lasting peace."

President Oner then said, "Amen to you, Mr. President. Also, the song you selected was my favorite. John Lennon and 'Imagine.' I love the Beatles' music. Do you remember the Beatles song 'Yellow Submarine'? It is my other favorite." With that they shook hands and President Oner left with his driver.

The only other people in the room were a few waiters who were assigned to the White House. The band was escorted from waiting outside to gather their equipment.

Chapter 14

The Recording

December 17, 2032

As he loaded his equipment, Les Mondo didn't pay much attention to the recorder he had left on at the White House dinner where he had just played with the band. He usually recorded every event and played it back to see if improvements were needed. No one had told him that what was going to be said was of great national concern and not to record the session. The small band had played only three songs before being asked to leave the room. There were seven singers present who sang one song in seven different languages, but they weren't known by any member of the band. It was an odd engagement for a band, but Les had been glad to get the work. Not many people played old songs, especially by John Lennon. He thought it was nice to meet the president and vice president, but Les Mondo thought both were real creepy dudes.

Money was tight for the small band; three of the four guys still lived with their parents. Only Les was married and required a steady income to survive. Everyone was hoping that the prestige of playing at the White House would launch their small band on a tour of the northeastern states. The band came from Youngstown, Ohio, and had another engagement the next night on the way back home.

Les and Leigh, his wife, had already concluded that if something didn't start to happen real soon, they would relocate to Texas and give up on the band. This was their last chance.

It was breakfast time on Sunday when Les let the last member of the band out at his house and headed for home himself. He lived about five minutes away and was ready to get some sleep.

It was about four in the afternoon when Les woke up. He was hungry. Leigh was not there; she was probably at her mom and dad's. Les thought he'd have a peanut butter and jelly sandwich with potato chips for dinner and breakfast at the same time. As he stuffed the sandwich into his mouth, he retrieved the tape recorder from his old Chevy van. Sitting in the living room chomping on potato chips, Les listened to the president talk to the seven world leaders at Friday's White House dinner.

Les couldn't believe his ears. What had he heard? He listened again to make sure. He thought, *I need to make another copy of this tape and hide the original.* He remembered where he used to hide his drugs before Leigh gave him an ultimatum: her or drugs. He had wisely chosen his beautiful wife and with a little help set the drugs aside.

After making a tape and hiding the original, Les thought, *What's next? If I turn in the president, I will be in serious trouble. If I don't say anything, everybody else will be in serious trouble.* About that time Leigh walked through the front door. "What's wrong with you, honey? You don't look too good. What's going on?"

Les replied, "I've got something for you to hear, but you can't tell anyone. You have to help me figure out what to do after you hear what I have."

Leigh's eyes were wide and filled with all kinds of emotions. She hollered at Les, "What is it? Tell me now."

As Les was starting the tape player, he kissed her and said, "I don't think we kissed hello yet." Leigh didn't respond. She didn't know what was happening, but was expecting something real bad.

After the tape was finished playing, Leigh asked, "What should we do?"

"I don't know—you tell me. Whatever it is, we have to figure it out real fast and do what we decide."

Leigh said, "I know: let's get in the van and go to Texas, and give it personally to the governor of Texas. He is the only person standing up to President Wiley and his deviousness."

"Do you think the governor will listen to us? He has to, or the world is really kaput." Both Leigh and Les sank into the old couch and looked bewildered. Les said, "Don't say nothing; just think for five minutes and then talk. We'll come up with a plan, and then we'll act. That's all I know right now. Except, could I be in trouble for recording the dinner? I wasn't told not to."

Leigh then said, "Let's be quiet for five minutes and then decide, okay?" Probably two minutes later, both started speaking at the same time. "We have to go to Texas."

Leigh added, "We can't tell a soul but the governor."

"Okay, when do we leave?"

Her reply was "We must leave now."

"How about your job? Are you scheduled to work tomorrow?"

Leigh had a look of determination on her face and said, "Honey, we may not be able to come back here again."

Les said, "We should go but we don't have enough money to make a trip to Texas".

"Yes we do," Leigh said. "I have a little saved for Christmas. My only concern is what to tell Mom and Dad."

"Let's tell them that I am trying to get a job in Texas and we both are going there, so you can see if you like it. Just say that and stick with that story. It's all we have. Do you want me to go over and tell them good-bye with you?"

Leigh said, "Yes, we may never be back again. Let's go now and then come by here and get a few things and go. Let's just go."

Les said, "We're both crazy, but let's do it."

By midnight Monday the couple had driven to Austin. They took turns driving and ate sandwiches and snacks on the way. Leigh downloaded information from the Internet and knew where the governor lived in Dripping Springs.

Les said, "Let's find a place to sleep and try to see Governor Hall in the morning."

Leigh was weary and mumbled, "Good. We will need to clean up before going to his house."

Les replied, "I guess so." Just outside Austin was an overnight camping place. They pulled in and slept in the back of the van.

There was a lot of noise outside, but neither Les nor Leigh heard much. It was almost noon before they woke up. Leigh said, "I still feel tired. It will take a few days to get over this trip."

"Me too," Les said. "Something else: we need to wash up before we meet Governor Hall."

Leigh said, "When I was a little girl, we would stay in these campsites. They have showers and bathrooms."

"Good. Let's find the shower. I'll stand guard while you shower, and then you come to the van to do your makeup while I shower. Keep the door locked until I get back. If anyone comes to the van, start it and honk the horn three times. Don't put your window down for any reason. I'm scared of the president finding out, and I'm a little scared of Texas, too."

Leigh had her shower, and it didn't take her very long to put on her makeup. She was very beautiful and didn't need much help to look better than she already did. The sun was out, and Leigh could see Les walking toward the van. At the same time they both saw a black sedan with government license plates driving slowly toward them. Should they run? What should they do? Inside were two men with cowboy hats on. They drove up to the van and stopped their car about the same time that Les was getting in the van. Both men opened their doors at the same time and stood outside the sedan looking at Les. The driver said to Les, "Sir, can you tell me if the showers have any hot water?"

Les looked horrified and replied in a squeaky voice, "Yes, the water is pretty warm."

The driver of the government sedan looked puzzled and said, "Thank you. Is everything all right with you all?"

Les then said, "Yes, everything is fine. I'm not used to taking a shower in the cold, with hot or cold water." The driver tipped his hat and smiled, saying, "I guess I will find the same as you just did. Have a good day, sir." Les waved good-bye and started the van, thinking, *Maybe I'm just a little paranoid. I hope that's all it is.*

You could see a Jack in the Box from the campsite. Les was still a little cautious but thought it was wise to be so under the conditions they both found themselves in. He said, "If we aren't followed and we don't see another government vehicle, I'll stop at Jack's to get us something to eat. I'm starving."

"Me too," Leigh said. "Turn right the next chance you get. We are pretty close to Dripping Springs." It wasn't very far down the road that they saw a sign saying, "Welcome to Dripping Springs, Texas, Home of Governor Jesse Hall." Les said, "I'm scared. Are you scared?"

"Yeah, I'm real scared. Whatever we do will probably change our lives forever, but we've got no choice."

Les smiled at his wife and said, "You are a pretty tough little girl. I am glad you're my wife, and whatever happens, as long as it's me and you, I will be just fine."

Leigh smiled and said, "Thanks, honey. I love you."

The road signs took them directly to the governor's house. By now it was nearly one in the afternoon on Tuesday. As they drove onto the property, a guard came from the security station and waved for them to stop the van. It was Buddy, the usual guard at the governor's residence. "Yes, sir, how I can help you folks? Are you lost?" Buddy said with a slow Texas drawl.

"No sir, we're not lost," Les said. "We both came from Ohio to see Governor Hall. It is very important that we get to see him."

"Okay, I understand, but let's take it one thing at a time," Buddy said as he looked over the couple. "Can you tell me what this is all about before I call the governor? Also do you have any weapons or explosives with you?"

Les said, "No, sir, we don't have nothing like that. Do you need to search us?"

Buddy said, "Maybe—we will see. First tell me what your business with Governor Hall is about."

Les replied, "Sir, I have a rock-and-roll band, and last Friday night I played at the White House. I record my sessions and play them after we finish. I recorded something President Wiley said that the governor needs to hear. I have the papers showing that I was invited to play at the White House. I'm not going to tell you anything else. You need to get the governor."

Buddy looked very serious and said, "What are your names?"

"I'm Les, and this is Leigh, my wife. Les and Leigh Mondo from Ohio."

"All right. Just come in and have a seat. I will call the good governor for you folks and you can have your visit." Buddy led them to the guard building and said, "I have some hot coffee if you would like a cup."

Both Les and Leigh said, "I would" at the same time.

They were all in the same room. Les and Leigh were getting a cup of coffee and Buddy was calling Governor Hall. When someone answered the phone, Buddy said, "Hey, Governor, you may want to meet a couple of young people from Ohio who drove down to see you. It could be important. I don't see a security risk. What do you want me to do, bring them to you or what?"

Governor Hall said, "Yes, lock the gate and bring them to the house." The governor met them at the door and invited them into his living room. "Buddy, come on in and tell me what is going on." Buddy explained briefly and passed the conversation on to Les. Les shared that he had a copy of a meeting that would change the world as it was known. Governor Hall asked if he had the tape with him. Leigh smiled and pulled an old recorder from her large purse. Les said it was a copy—he had hidden the original—but the sound quality was pretty good. Governor Hall said, "Let's go into my study and hear the tape. Buddy, thanks for taking care of this. I will talk to you later."

Leigh prepared the tape so the governor could hear it. She handed him an ear bud and said, "Use this; it works better." The room was silent for a long time. The governor didn't move, and his face didn't show any expression. He just sat and listened.

Finally the governor had heard the complete tape. He looked at the young couple sitting in his study and said, "This changes everything; this will change the course of many people's lives, including yours. What are your plans for the future?"

Leigh said, "Before this happened, we were thinking about relocating to Texas and trying to get some sort of work. When this happened, we had to fast-forward our plans."

The governor said, "I don't think you should go back to Ohio. I don't think you broke any laws, but the way the country is, you never know. You will be safe in Texas. Why don't you stay here with us for a few days and let the state of Texas adopt you as new citizens? I'm sure there is work you can do. I will make a few calls. In the meantime, enjoy your visit with us. I would like to get to know you both better anyway. My wife, Ellie, daughter and mother –in- law is in Austin till this afternoon, but I will introduce you to my dad and he will show you around our farm. Just make yourself at home; I need to make some calls that are very urgent. I'm sure you understand. Also please keep this quiet.

"Something else: if you need to get some of your belongings from Ohio, I can take care of that from here. I don't think you should leave Texas, period."

Les said, "We sort of figured we would be staying. Whoever goes to Ohio and retrieves our stuff, could I have one person who would be responsible for the original tape? In time it could be a very important part of history."

Chapter 15

Ransom for Freedom

Tuesday, December 21, 2032

Governor Hall remained in his office to make calls to Howard Martin and Clint Ross. The first to answer the phone was Clint. "Hey, buddy, I know it's close to Christmas, but you and Howard need to come over to my house ASAP. I've got some news that can't wait."

Clint said, "Okay, I'm on my way. Give me thirty minutes."

"Good," said Jesse. "I'll try Howard again. I think he's trying to call me back now. See you soon."

On the other end of the phone Howard said, "Hi, Jesse. What's up?"

Jesse said, "Howard, I've got something that can't wait. Clint is on the way over, and I need to see both of you immediately."

Both Howard and Clint arrived just about three thirty in the afternoon; Buddy waved them through the gate. Jesse met both at the door and said, "I'm sorry to intrude on your time like this, but this can't wait. Come on in to the study." Once all three men were seated, Jesse told them to look out the large window and see his guest. He explained the story and told them to listen to the tape. Nothing more was said. All three men were intently interested in what the president had said to the seven world leaders the previous Friday night at the White House.

Howard was the first to speak. "I'm not surprised by this at all. We were heading in this direction. It may serve our purpose well.

For instance, we don't have to leave the Union. We can continue as an American state, independent from the corrupt federal government. I believe this could be a way for Hal Wilson to properly assume his position as president. At the same time, I think we should maintain very strong independent states' rights. Perhaps we should separate ourselves until the Union returns to the original constitutional government as it was first intended."

Clint said, "We need a plan. I can see where this will take us. We may not secede from the Union, but it will be the same as if we did secede from the Union. We can't imagine the issues we will have once we separate ourselves from the federal government, but we have no choice."

Jesse listened until both spoke briefly and then said, "Men, this is the worst news for America that one could ever hear. After two hundred and fifty years the government will give away our nation. Can you imagine that? Give it away. Look how many men have died for our freedom. Then one day an idiot president will just give it away. He will do this because of a deluded belief system that is in control of this country. Texas doesn't have a choice but to express or declare its own individual states' rights. Once we become independent, we will experience many pains of separation. We will be separated from both the Union and the world.

"This is our plan. We will notify President Wiley and advise him that we have a recording of the meeting he had last Friday night. If need be, we will e-mail him a transcript of every word spoken. We will then give Mr. Wiley option one or option two. Option one: the federal government gives Texas a hundred billion dollars in gold bullion. We will send Texas Air National Guard planes to Fort Knox or wherever to receive the gold. Wiley will have only three hours to agree on option one. Option two is to broadcast onEBN on the late night news. If this news leaks, he might be jailed. It could ruin his plans. It could help Texas get a fresh start.

"This is the best part: once the planes have delivered the gold to Texas, we will go on ENB anyway. This just might cause the people of

America to wake up. I think that Texas has a real opportunity to be as she once was, great. Let's give her a chance."

Clint said, "Wow. I'm in. This has caused us to act and quit vacillating. We need to decide who will lead the state of Texas as president. I vote for Jesse. Do I have a second?"

Howard said, "Yes, sir, I second your motion. Jesse, you are the president of the New America. We will either do something great or we will all be hanged together."

Jesse smiled and said, "One or the other is inevitable. Men, wait here. I'm going to ask Leigh if she can type. I would like to get this transcript as soon as possible." Leigh said that she could help with the transcript; it would take about an hour. The three men let Leigh have the study to work and went to the den to formulate their plans.

"Howard, have you gathered information about the secretary of defense?" Jesse asked. "I'm thinking that as soon as it's feasible, we should include him in our plans. He should be back in Texas for Christmas. The New America will have one secretary of defense who serves directly under me. Also, both you guys will be my advisers. Then the chief justice of the Supreme Court will be my council. As soon as Texas can draft a constitution and maintain its own economy and security, we will elect a proper president. The people need to understand this. As soon as Leigh completes the transcript, we will send it to the president. Clint, do you have any information about establishing our own currency? Do you have any idea how much gold and silver is in Texas at the present time?"

"Yes, I do have some encouraging information about the amounts of gold and silver in Texas," Clint said. "I was surprised to find out that many banks and large investment corporations have large sums of both gold and silver. Even the small investors throughout Texas should have somewhere in the neighborhood of four or five trillion dollars. Once we nationalize gold and silver, the state should be in a position to maintain a fairly strong economy."

Jesse said, "Howard, call Captain Smith and have him ready. We need to find out how many planes are needed to carry that much gold.

We also need to have a way of determining if we're getting real gold and silver. Wiley may try to make fools out of us and give us painted lead or something else."

Soon Leigh brought each of the men a copy of the words that had been spoken. Jesse thanked her and said, "Men, it is really time to cut bait. I will call the president. If he agrees, we will have a few hours to get the gold and silver. Let's get the planes on standby."

By now it was five thirty in the evening Texas time, which was six thirty White House time. Jesse sighed and said, "Here goes. You both pray while I talk to the president."

President Wiley was having a late dinner with some close friends when the phone rang. He was told it was the governor of Texas. Annoyed, he thought, *This can't be good. What does he want with me at this late hour?* He excused himself from his dinner party, saying to his guests, "Please excuse me for just a moment. I will be back soon." Taking the call in the Oval Office, President Wiley picked up the phone and said, "Yes, Governor, this is President Wiley. Can I help you?"

Governor Hall hadn't expected a friendly greeting and didn't receive one. "Mr. Wiley, last Friday night you hosted the leaders of seven of the most powerful countries in the world. At this meeting you shared your plan and immediate intentions to vacate America for a one-world order. I can give you a transcript of every word said at this meeting if you like. I believe if the people of America knew how evil you are, they might force a change—a needed change for the better. I will give you a choice. One choice is that you can somehow pay Texas a hundred billion dollars in gold bullion and continue your plan. The other is that the transcript will be on the ten o'clock news tonight. Your call."

President Wiley said, "Governor, you caught me off guard. I don't know how you managed to get that information, but it sounds accurate. I need to sort this out and discuss this with Gerald. You now have me at a great disadvantage. I need to sort out my options."

Governor Hall said, "You have only two options. It is six thirty at the White House. I need an answer within the hour. I will let you consider your options, and if I don't hear from you the transcripts will be made public by eight thirty. I will not make contact with you. If I don't hear from you, we do option two immediately." With that last remark by Governor Hall, both men hung up the phone.

Before returning to his waiting dinner guests, President Wiley called Gerald Cunningham. Per their usual practice Gerald was soon on his way to help in any way possible. As the evening progressed, the president seemed to be somewhat disconnected from his guests and their conversation. It would take Gerald close to thirty minutes to arrive at the White House; the president would excuse himself for more-urgent matters.

"Folks, I just received a call a short time ago, and I need to be excused from our dinner. I am grateful to all of you for coming over and spending a little time together. Sometimes these things happen. It's not anything of national concern, but it is a matter that requires my immediate attention." After saying that, President Wiley left the room, shaking a few hands on the way out.

Gerald was already sitting in the Oval Office, waiting. The president entered the room, sat down, unwrapped a cigar, and nervously began chomping on the end. "Gerald, I don't see a way out of this dilemma. Somehow we have to get a hundred billion in gold to Texas. He will probably turn us in anyway, but what choice do we have?

"I don't know what worldwide repercussions this could cause. It could and most likely would reverberate throughout the world. I know eventually we will win, but this could set us back for several years. It could cause riots and unrest. This issue is extremely unsettling. Most of our decisions are planned, and the events run their planned course. This time the events are running us."

Gerald spoke up, "Sir, usually the cause determines our actions. This is no different. Our plans may be derailed, but we have to stay on course. Extenuating circumstances may alter our course, but we have to continue. Whatever the cost, we must continue going forward. I do believe Texas will try to deter us in any way they can. Ultimately we are in a battle of ideas. Our ideas are best for everyone and will win out in the end. So, my friend and my president, give Texas the money and let's be prepared for what's next. But as soon as the news hits the airways, we will again surrender our cause to the world. It could work in our favor; I really believe it is time for everybody to be equal. The cause is greater than we are."

It was very close to eight thirty when the president called the governor of Texas and told him he would pay the ransom. He advised Governor Hall that although the arrangements weren't complete, they would be within one or two hours. He then called the secretary of the treasury, Herman Butler, and told him to prepare $100 billion in gold bullion for the state of Texas. Mr. Butler informed the president that he wasn't authorized to make such a payment. It needed the approval of Congress or a preapproved emergency funding order from Congress. Gerald told Herman Butler to get the money ready; he would have the approval within minutes. He knew he could call in some favors from a few senior members of Congress. If he could pull this off, then both the president and vice president would be obligated to a few men who wanted to be in the new inner circle of world leadership. Most of the members of Congress didn't understand the particulars, but almost everyone knew of President Wiley's intentions. For the last few months America and the world had been noticing the intentions of the G22 Conference. President Wiley exercised more power than any president before him. In all his plans and schemes, he never asked for money. He did spend money and mandated his way through any obstacle that arose. His action was designed to consolidate and strengthen his power and diminish the legislative branch of the federal government.

It took seven congressmen in a special secret meeting to approve Texas's ransom. This was done by ten in the evening on Tuesday, December 21. The seven men knew that what they were doing was in their best personal interests in the long run.

Chapter 16

The Transfer

December 21, 2032

All three men anxiously waited for the phone to bring them news from the White House. Right at 10:00 p.m. Eastern Standard Time the phone rang. As he briefly spoke to President Wiley, the governor nodded. Upon hanging up, he said, "I can't believe it. "He said the arrangements are complete."

Howard said, "While you were on the phone to President Wiley, I figured the approximate weight. A hundred billion dollars' worth of gold will weigh eight hundred and sixty-three tons—that is, if gold is around thirty-six hundred dollars per ounce. I don't know the rate of silver, but we need at least nine large transport planes just for that amount of gold. The next question is where we safely store that much."

Governor Hall said, "Before the gold arrives, we will have access to bank vaults. We will then have the Texas Forty-Ninth Armored Division move and secure the gold in the proper bank vaults. Along with that, we'll have the Texas Rangers maintain security. They won't have enough men, but they can assume the responsibility and use the Forty-Ninth for the actual security.

"Once the gold is in Texas, we will need to meet with senior officials in the state government. Somehow we need to separate the New America from the state of Texas. Once the New America gets on solid ground, we can form the new government. I really believe everyone will support us. Given the events that have happened over the last few days, I don't see any other way."

Clint said, while looking at his notes, "Men, we must move fast and be decisive. As a sovereign state we choose not to be connected to a universal one-world government. We are now forced to separate Texas from the national government. As this unfolds, we shouldn't have very much opposition. The government of Texas will remain intact as it is now. As leaders of this state, we will be forced to act in the best interests of Texas. We will form a quasi-government. This will give us a lot of latitude in moving forward without interference from Texas or anything else. The more effective and competent Texas becomes, the more political forces will challenge and try our authority.

"In time the government of Texas will be the new federal government of the New America. Since we will have only one state in the new government, we won't need a federal bureaucracy. If we ever have other states join us in a federation of states, we will need a federal government. In other words, everything that we do to separate ourselves from the federal government will be done as a sovereign state operating under the Declaration of Independence, for the sole purpose of reestablishing the original Constitution of the United States of America.

"I would like to say that if and when other states join with Texas as one nation, each state should have its own separate constitution. This time, limit the federal government and specify its purpose and duties. My reason is that Texas may declare God as our Lord and Savior. Another state may declare Hinduism as their recognized religion. It will be up to each state to determine what laws and regulations will be approved and observed by their citizens without interference from a national government.

"There are many issues that we should try to resolve before we're confronted with them. It will seem like a monumental task to solve the many problems that will immediately rise up once we separate ourselves from the federal government. Because of this most recent development, we are handed a gift. Even without this gift of a hundred billion dollars, we are still handed a gift. The gift is that Texas now has a chance to prosper on its own and is forced to do so.

"As I speak my mind, please don't hesitate to interject your thoughts if you don't agree. We will have only one chance to get this right, and we all need to be on the same page."

Apparently Clint had already prepared notes for discussion for when they would meet after Christmas. He hadn't realized that some of his notes would be used as a guide for immediate action. As he reviewed his notes, he added other remarks and jotted them down as he continued to explain his thoughts and views.

Clint continued, "If America becomes part of a unified one-world order, the military bases in Texas will either be vacated or occupied by NATO. This could be a grave problem for a new country. It can't be addressed now, but it is a great concern. The secretary of defense and the chairman of the Joint Chief of Staff live in and are from Texas. As we move along with our plans, we need to include the military leaders. It is hard to say what they will do when America is dissolved. I hope some of the military forces will join with us to continue freedom. The navy has seven fleets. If they all come to Texas, we will be overwhelmed. At the same time, this would be a great opportunity for Texas and the New America to strengthen its navy. We now have a formidable coast guard. If we could have an aircraft carrier and one or two submarines, we would have a formidable navy force. With all the bases we now have in Texas, we would be in pretty good shape. If we have too large an operating military complex, our budget will never be balanced. As a new nation, we must stay in balance. We could receive all the ships and decommission them to keep the cost down, and then we could commission them as funds are available and as the ships are needed. I would hope that our secretary of defense would help any state that separates itself from the new world order.

"We should immediately notify Hal Wilson so he can respond as he may need to. He is operating from California. I would think that as a state, California would go with President Wiley and the new one-world order. This would leave Hal Wilson without a place to establish his presidency. That could be a sticky issue if he wants to come to Texas. I don't have an answer for that problem right now; we will need to think about that later on.

"The military will be responsible for distributing food. At present Texas exports more than seventy percent of the meat and produce it produces. Our number-one concern is providing adequate food for the people of Texas. All the federal farms and processing plants will be nationalized immediately. Any surplus food will be stored and managed for our citizens. Eventually we may have trade relations with other states. That is why we will store as much foodstuffs as possible. The planting, raising, harvesting, and processing will continue without any interruption.

"Hospitals and clinics will be required to operate as usual. Each city that has a hospital or clinic will have an office that answers directly to the mayor. The mayor will have access to the state so as to maintain the best of care for its citizens during these times of change.

"All the electricity-generating plants will operate at maximum capabilities. During these times everyone can use their electricity as desired. Any coal plants that are now closed but can be used will be put back in service. All public utility companies will operate as usual; water, telephone, gas, and the Internet will stay in service.

"Each municipality will continue to operate as needed to maintain city services and keep the people safe. For every hundred dollars we send to the federal government, we get twenty-three dollars returned to Texas in some form. Once we get a handle on operating independently, we should prosper as a state.

"Something we need to be mindful of: if we join up with several states and return to an organized federal government too soon, it could cause Texas great problems. Some states may not be self-supporting. Some states have separate Indian nations within their states. It could be like two different states. Our concern should be for Texas to be strong and independent first and foremost. Then we could proceed slowly and cautiously as it suits Texas.

"This could be the most difficult part. As we implement a new government, the people will be very cautious and suspicious. Political groups, the unions, and especially the business community will cease to operate as before. Each group will do everything in their power to gain any advantage. Each group will need to be neutralized. Remember Shays' Rebellion in 1786. Because of the massive war debt, this group ended up paying more in taxes than everyone else. Someone had to pay, and it was the farmers. Speculators took advantage of the farmers' debt, and the federal government didn't or couldn't help."

It was eleven at night; in Texas, the governor's phone rang. Jesse answered, "Governor Hall."

"Governor, this is Vernon Wiley. As we speak, the aircraft is being loaded with the gold. I don't know how long it will take to arrive in Texas. I was told it would be delivered to the naval air station in Fort Worth. I hope you keep your part of the agreement." With that, President Wiley hung up the phone.

Jesse said, "The planes are being loaded. Howard, call the Texas Rangers and have as many Rangers as possible report to the base in Fort Worth. Have the planes park in a remote area of the base. Also arrange transportation and overnight accommodations for the aircraft crew at the base, have the base commander return them to where they came from, or let them wait for the planes after they're unloaded.

"Clint, call Captain Smith and have him take as many men as possible to secure the planes. Don't tell anyone what is on the planes. Just have them guard and protect the planes, and make sure we can get in the planes tomorrow morning. Also call John Williams, the adjutant general of the Texas State Guard, and tell him to dispatch a company of soldiers to help guard the planes. Also tell Captain Smith when everybody arrives at the air base that the Texas Rangers will be in charge of this operation. Tell him to keep the governor's office informed hourly.

"I'll call the director of the Public Safety Commission now and have him meet us at the capitol building as soon as possible. He is responsible for emergency management, homeland security, and several agencies that will help us do what is needed to secure Texas."

It was nearly three in the morning when the governor's cell phone rang at the capitol building. He was having a closed-door meeting with

Edwin Roberts, the director of Texas's public safety commission. It was Captain Smith, the trooper in charge of the governor's personal security. He had gone to Fort Worth to be the eyes for the governor. "Hey, Governor, the planes have landed. The Rangers and soldiers have secured the planes, and security is established. As you requested, I viewed the contents of each plane. There are nine planes with several special pallets of gold in each one. The air force pilot gave me the planes' shipping manifest. It reads that they shipped 1,786,000 pounds of gold. I removed the cover on a few pallets, and it sure looked like gold. I cut several bars with my knife and it was solid."

"Thanks, Ray. Get some sleep. You will be very busy tomorrow."

Chapter 17

The Lone Star State

Thursday, December 23, 2032

After the conversation with Captain Smith, Governor Hall was satisfied that Texas now had $100 billion in gold. It was nearly four thirty in the morning, and the governor was exhausted. He would turn in for the night and try to be rested for the challenges of the upcoming day. His trusted leaders, Clint Ross and Howard Martin, would do as much as possible to have all the involved officials and military leaders be at the state capitol at one o'clock on Wednesday. They would be briefed on the current situation and assigned different duties to ensure security and make sure everything went as smoothly as possible. Arrangements were made for the Federal Reserve Bank in Dallas to receive the gold. It would be guarded by the Texas Rangers. Upon arrival of the huge shipment of gold at the Federal Reserve Bank, someone there would verify that the shipment was actually gold. The Texas Rangers would also prevent any physical transfer of assets from the Federal Reserve Bank.

Early Wednesday afternoon, Governor Hall arrived at the capitol building promptly at one o'clock. He met with Clint and Howard briefly and privately before the meetings were to start. His second meeting would be with Neville Crow, the secretary of defense, at one fifteen. Jesse conveyed to Clint and Howard some negative possibilities they might encounter with the secretary of defense and the many military installations that were stationed in Texas. Ruby, the governor's secretary, was not working this day. When the brief meeting was over, Jesse went to the door and opened it to see if Secretary Crow had arrived. He was quietly sitting outside the governor's office. "Mr. Secretary, please come on in."

As Mr. Crow entered the room, both Clint and Howard stood up to shake his hand. Jesse knew that everyone knew each other. After each man greeted Mr. Crow, Jesse said, "Let's sit down and get to business."

Secretary Crow said, "Jesse, I hope you have a very good reason for asking all of the military commanders in Texas to be here today."

"Yes sir. Here is a transcript of a very secret meeting held at the White House last Friday. Present at this meeting were leaders of seven of the largest countries in the world plus President Wiley. At this meeting President Wiley announced a decision and encouraged quick implementation of a new one-world government. He was received well by the seven world leaders, and his plans for implementation were generally accepted by everyone. I have a tape recording of the meeting, and I just handed you a word-for-word transcript.

"Sir, in the very near future, America will be handed over, and nothing can or will be done to stop President Wiley. We believe that at this time in history, Texas has no choice but to separate itself from the federal government."

As Jesse handed the transcript to Secretary Crow, he sat motionless with a steely, angry look on his face. It didn't take Secretary Crow long to read and understand the gravity of the situation. After reading the transcript, Secretary Crow said, "Men, I serve the United States of America. I can't imagine doing what this president plans on doing. Considering the worldwide situation, he can probably do whatever he wants. I don't know what to say. Texas may be doing what is best for Texas. My question is what is best for the country—that is, if we have a country.

"Men, I don't want any of my base commanders to meet here today. It could be construed as treason. Governor Hall, did you know that more than half of the base commanders are foreign and have been assigned by the United Nations? I will have a meeting with the chairman of the Joint Chiefs of Staff and we will try to get a handle on this situation. I was notified about this meeting and advised all the commanders to forgo it." It seemed as if Secretary Crow was trying to sort out the situation as he spoke. He continued, "Men, it's been a longtime policy of this administration and previous administrations to use foreign commanders to command statewide bases. They also use our commanders to command foreign bases.

"It would be very plausible for NATO to make a few key transfers and almost overnight NATO would be in control of all the world's military bases." Secretary Crow's face was red; his anger was obvious. He said, "Men, we're screwed. Have you thought about the fact that when Texas separates from America, NATO forces could occupy the state's many bases? This could jeopardize the sovereign rights of Texas."

Clint spoke up. "If we are occupied by a foreign power, we will isolate each base. We will destroy all roads and highways leading to each one. We will cut off all their utilities. Any Texan serving in a foreign military installation in Texas will be ordered to report to the Texas National Guard for reassignment. Mr. Crow, I hope we stay in close communication and that Texas is the birthplace of a new America." Secretary Crow stood up to shake each man's hand and then abruptly left the room. Once outside he could see several of his commanders standing by. As Mr. Crow left the building, he had his aide notify his commanders that the meeting wouldn't take place.

The governor, Howard, and Clint spent all afternoon meeting with different groups who would be involved in forming a transitional government. Several of the state legislators were apprehensive about how the state government was being superseded by a temporary new federal government. Governor Hall did everything he could to alleviate any fears they harbored. He assured them that as Texas became secure, a new constitution would be in place. At the end of the day everyone understood what had to be done. Nobody knew that freedom would be forced on Texas.

All the various state agencies and the Texas State Guard were making preparations to secure Texas from the outside world. The actual date hadn't been set. The adjutant general of the Texas Guard had advised the new transitional government that they didn't have enough manpower to secure all the borders. In a meeting with Governor Hall, John Williams, the adjutant general of Texas State Guard, suggested that the governor nationalize the Border Patrol. They had the ability and tools to secure the border with Mexico, but the federal government had placed many restrictions on the agency.

By now it was nearly six thirty on Thursday, the day before Christmas Eve. Several reporters were gathered at the capitol building. They had heard many different rumors and were hoping that a story would break at any minute. Jesse, Clint, and Howard were about to try to have some sort of Christmas with their families, but in their hearts they knew differently. Jesse said, "Men, let's try to go home again. So far I believe we've done all we can do for the Lone Star State and for New America."

Chapter 18

Christmas 2032

Christmas was quiet and somewhat private. By now Les and Leigh were part of the family. Becky had gotten a job in San Antonio and moved in with her grandmother Lenore, and the two of them had come to the Alamo for the holidays. As Christmas dinner was being set, Orville mentioned, "What about the guards at the gate? What are they going to do for Christmas dinner?"

Ellie smiled and said, "I guess you need to invite them in for dinner." Soon the house was filled with people and the wonderful aromas of Christmas dinner. Three tables were crowded together to hold the food. As everyone filled their plates and took a seat, Orville stood up. "Instead of a prayer, Les would like to sing something special for this wonderful Christmas dinner. I believe it will be more than sufficient."

Les stood up and looked to the ceiling and began to sing "O Holy Night." After finishing his song Les sat down. No one hurried to eat. The moment was too solemn, and everyone was still savoring something very special that they had felt by everyone hearing that great song. Perhaps it was the aroma from the food, but before long, the quiet left and everyone had more than their fill.

Sunday at the Alamo was always special, there was a lot of food left over from Christmas dinner. Usually nothing planned, but often several neighbors, sometimes friends from Orville's old church, came by and they had a church service. Somewhere between nine thirty and eleven the service would start. Sometimes they gathered in the guard shack, sometimes the house or on the porch. Wherever it was, it was always relaxed and special. Everyone visited and had coffee until they felt like no one else was coming over. Sometimes they only sang hymns and prayed.

This Sunday, Buddy wanted to share, and had printed a few Scriptures for everyone to discuss. Les volunteered to sing a special song before the Bible study began and sang "Great Is Thy Faithfulness." Afterward, Buddy said, "Les, you have a special way of singing. I know your future may seem cloudy, but the truth is, your future is very bright. Leigh and Les, you are just where you need to be, and God will provide."

Everybody said, "Amen."

Les said, "I feel like I need to share something with you all. Leigh and I, well, we have never gone to church. Where we come from, church is something the old people do. I don't know anything about the Bible, but in these few days Leigh and I have seen how important everybody's faith is to them. It's your life. We've talked to Orville a lot, and he's helping us understand. For the first time in my life I tried to read the Bible. I'm sorry to say this, but it is hard to understand. We want to understand. Orville let me borrow an old hymnbook. I started reading the words to those great songs, and both Leigh and I began to understand a little. We both want to be Christians." With that everybody went to both Leigh and Les to hug them. Eventually Buddy shared a few special Scriptures, and then everyone had leftover Christmas dinner.

Every Sunday afternoon for many, many years, Orville and Jesse had taken a nap between one thirty and three o'clock. Orville would nap in the living room and Jesse in the study. The living room was out because several people were already camped out there watching TV. This particular Sunday was warmer than usual, and Orville used the front porch. It was not the best choice, but it would work. As Jesse sat on the couch in the study to take off his shoes, his cell phone rang. He thought to himself, *There goes my nap.* It was Neville Crow on the line.

"Hello, Governor, this is Neville Crow."

Jesse said, "Hello, Mr. Secretary. It's good to hear from you."

"Jesse, I'm flying back to Washington this afternoon and I need to meet with you before leaving. This is extremely important, and I insist that we meet before I leave."

"Neville, I'm at my house, but we can meet anywhere you choose."

"Thanks, Jesse. How about your office in forty-five minutes?"

"I'll be there. Is this a private meeting or can I invite Clint and Howard?"

The secretary replied, "Jesse, it's a top-secret meeting. I would like for it to be between just you and me, but after the meeting you will need to share the information with Howard and Clint."

Jesse replied, "Yes, sir. I'm on my way."

Ellie wasn't surprised when Jesse told her he needed to go to his office. She kissed him good-bye and smiled. As she walked Jesse to the front door, she said, "Honey, if you run for governor again, I won't vote for you."

This Sunday there were two guards on duty at the guard shack. Usually on Sunday there was only one on duty, but because it was a holiday, there were two guards to handle the tourist crowd, if needed. As Jesse entered the guard shack, he said, "Men, I hate to disturb your Sunday afternoon, but I need to go to the office."

Buddy was still on duty and replied, "I'll take you, sir; I was getting a little bored anyway."

As Jesse got in his vehicle, he said, "Buddy, I'll sit in the back. I need to make a few calls, and you need to call ahead and let security know we need to access the building. Also let them know that Neville Crow, the secretary of defense, will need to be escorted to my office." Buddy smiled back toward the governor, gave him a salute, and said, "Yes, sir."

One the way Jesse called his friends Clint and Howard. He apologized for the intrusion and then told them that they both needed to meet with him after he met with the secretary of defense. Both men understood and knew duty was of the utmost importance and would be there.

As Buddy drove Jesse's vehicle into the capitol parking lot, Crow's vehicle arrived as well. He was in a chauffeured vehicle accompanied by an escort vehicle. *How impressive,* Jesse thought to himself. By now there were several capitol police officers in place for security. Jesse was glad. *We don't need to take any chances on security, and often I am way too lax about security.*

Once in the governor's office, the men shook hands. Neville smiled and said, "It is very good to see you, Jesse. You need to sit down. What I'm about to tell you may rock your boat a little." Jesse didn't have a clue about what was next, but he was a little nervous and returned a faint smile.

Sitting down, Jesse said, "Yes, sir. I hope you bring good news to Texas—my state and still your state. We need good news."

Neville then said, "Jesse, I hope I have good news for Texas and America. Last Thursday when we met, I purposely acted surprised when I read the transcript of President Wiley's meeting. Actually, I already knew about that meeting. You did a great service for our country by providing evidence of Wiley's deceitful plot. It was extremely important that you didn't know what we knew. The reason is that we've ordered all our base commanders overseas to come home immediately. All military personnel in India, China, and Russia have been evacuated to a safe place. As we speak, all foreign commanders and enlisted personnel stationed on American bases are being dismissed, with orders to vacate American soil.

"About two years ago, Robert Schultz and I were having a beer and talking about old times. After several beers, I asked Robert if he knew that the United States was going down the tube. He became very serious, and from that meeting we started a conversation that ended up being a plan. Since then we've added several other leaders, four senators, and six congressmen. These are very influential men who, like Robert and me, will die for America. Our hands were tied until the Supreme Court overruled the Constitution and gave the presidency to Mr. Wiley, but that wasn't quite enough. When he had his secret meeting at the White House a couple of weeks ago, that sealed his fate.

"There still remain many issues that need to be resolved. If we installed Hal Wilson as president, America would be intact as a nation, but the country would be so weak that in the next election, the progressives would be back in office. The only way America can survive is by having a housecleaning.

This is the plan; it will be acted on this January 1, 2033. President Wiley and Vice President Gerald Cunningham will be at Camp David during this time for something—I'm not really sure. At Camp David both men will be relieved of their duties and kept under house arrest. At the same time all nine members of the Supreme Court will be discharged from further service. We will immediately meet with all the cabinet members to advise them of the emergency measures in place to regain America. We will assure them that we have a strong grip on all branches of the military, the FBI, the CIA, and the Border Patrol. We hope that each cabinet member will realize that this is our last opportunity to restore America to its previous greatness.

"If the cabinet members submit and comply with the new government, we will immediately begin our changes. At the first meeting, we will explain as clearly as possible that we are the new government. We have three goals: the first is to restore constitutional government as outlined in the Constitution, the second is to let America thrive on its own by getting the government out of America's way of life, and the third is to strengthen the states and weaken the federal government. If any cabinet member refuses to participate, he or she will be removed immediately. At the first meeting you will be introduced as America's acting president.

"These are a few of the changes that need to happen for America to have a chance at recovery. Senators will be able to serve only one term of six years. The term for members of the House of Representatives will be two three-year terms. So immediately any senator who has held a seat for more than six years will be let out to pasture. The same goes for the House.

"There are many issues that need to be visited: abortion rights, gay rights, prayer in school. It is now a federal offense for citizens to own a gun. This is a federal issue. It is a citizen's constitutional right to bear firearms, and this will be corrected.

"The sworn duty of the Supreme Court justices and federal judges is only to interpret the law, not legislate law. Before seating a new Supreme Court or any new federal judge, this law will be defined and sworn upon. Future justices can and will be impeached for violating this clearly defined law.

"America's involvement in the United Nations will be terminated. They will need to move their operations to another country. We understand when we pull away from the UN that a vacuum will be created. Many terrorist organizations will try to take advantage of our withdrawing. We will still support our rightful causes, but it will be on America's terms.

"America will not participate in the G22 Summit; this organization's interests are not in keeping with the best interests of America.

"Foreign aid will be used only to support our friends and allies. Any foreign aid will be temporary and limited.

"All the American borders will be secured. It will be very difficult for any undocumented worker to find employment. Illegal aliens will find themselves in a hostile country. America will no longer provide any benefits to illegal aliens as we have done in the past. Anyone hiring an undocumented worker will be heavily fined. This will be enforced with stiff measures.

"The federal Environmental Protection Agency will be closed. It will be a state-run entity. Each state will do what is best for its own state, without any federal funding or federal interference.

"The president will not have any legislative abilities, by using mandates or executive privilege. The only legislative ability will be the War Powers Resolution as outlined in the Constitution, although the resolution will need to be better defined and enforced.

"Any bill or amendment that is presented to Congress by a committee must have an up-or-down vote during the session of Congress to which it is presented. Both houses must develop a reasonable method of presenting a bill or amendment and completing its work by an up-or-down vote. One method is that no new bill can be voted on until previous bills are voted on.

"As it now stands, the federal government owns property throughout our land. All federal land and property will be returned to each state that it is now on.

"The income tax system now in place will be replaced by a flat tax system. Everyone will pay sixteen percent. This will reduce the biggest bureaucratic organization in the world, the IRS, by ninety percent.

"There will be no unions for federal workers. Government workers will be paid as much as nonfederal workers, but not more. Also, there will be a federal right-to-work law. This will weaken the unions' stranglehold on our national growth and vitality.

"Social Security will be independently managed by outside investment organizations.

"Government health care has failed miserably for all its citizens. Somehow, someway, the federal government will loosen this stranglehold on America. The health care industry will be turned back to doctors and the insurance companies. And doctors won't have the limits and restrictions they now have.

"The federal government has many government agencies and bureaus that need to be reviewed and done away with.

"Most universities and colleges receive millions from the federal government. Most students do receive a good education, but at the same time, they are taught to hate America and its liberty. The federal government won't subsidize these schools anymore—or any schools for that matter. They are not the government's responsibility. They never should have been.

"There is a branch of the government that has more influence than all other branches together. It is the press. I said 'branch of government' facetiously No one should restrict the freedom of the press, but every political story will be required to have the opposing side's view. Neither side will like this, but it will put them all on the same playing field. The result will be that truthful articles are published.

"I believe we have a chance to turn America around. The committee would like you to be acting president. Our plan is to manage America for four years. We will write laws that will be in force for twenty-five years. This should give America enough time to recover.

"Jesse, I need to catch a plane, but here is my cell phone number. Call when you have an answer."

Jesse said, "Sir, the cause is greater than any consideration I may have. Of course I will serve." By now both men were standing. Secretary Crow reached out to shake Jesse's hand and said, "Mr. President, let's give America one more chance."

Chapter 19

Mr. Hall Goes to Washington

In less than one hour, Jesse Hall had gone from being governor of Texas to president of the United States. The capitol police notified Clint and Howard that the meeting was over. As they walked toward the governor's office, both men noticed that several federal police officers were guarding the governor's office and the general area. They didn't know if that was bad or good; it looked bad.

Jesse started talking as soon as the men entered the room; he didn't give them a chance to sit down. He told the story in the same order in which Secretary Crow had told it to him. Both Clint and Howard sat motionless and in awe as the story unfolded. When Jesse shared that he was now the president of the United States of America, Clint, smiling, merely said, "Can we keep the gold?" Jesse laughed and said that since it was in a federal bank, they probably had possession of the money.

"Men, I need you both with me in Washington, Howard as the attorney general and you, Clint, as secretary of state."

Both men said, "Yes, Mr. President" at the same time, with big smiles on their faces.

"Also I need both of you to stop all the measures we put in place to separate Texas from the federal government. Call John Williams and Edwin Roberts and tell them to put everything on hold. I will notify Chief Justice William Carney. Clint, you may need to stay in Texas to make sure everything goes smoothly. As soon as you get everything under control, come to Washington."

Jesse finished speaking with Clint and Howard and left for home. He couldn't wait to see the reaction on Ellie's face when he broke the news to her. He thought it better to tell only Ellie and his dad. It was close to six o'clock when Jesse arrived at the Alamo. As he walked into the house, Ellie was reading something. She looked up and said, "What's going on? Why are you grinning from ear to ear?"

"I've got something very important to tell you, but it needs to be kept quiet for a few days. Let's go to the bedroom and I'll tell you everything." Jesse reached for Ellie's hand and led her to the bedroom. "Honey, I will tell you everything just as it was told to me." Then Jesse told Ellie everything in the same manner as Secretary Crow had told him. Ellie lay across the bed motionless while Jesse told her the story. As the story unfolded, Ellie knew it would have a big ending but didn't expect this one. Jesse ended by saying, "Ellie, honey, I am the new president of the United States of America."

Ellie's jaw dropped, and she placed both hands over her mouth in shock. She said, "I can't believe what you just told me. You went to town as governor of Texas and came back as the president of the United States. Honey, what are we going to do?"

Jesse was softly rubbing her arm, and said, "Somehow, someway, we are going to try to be a part of returning America to its glory."

The next day as Jesse got into his vehicle to head to the airport, he noticed several reporters with TV cameras. Usually Jesse walked to the shack and boarded there. This time the reporters were kept outside the gate and Jesse was picked up at the house, which was about 150 feet from the guard shack. As he entered the SUV, several of the reporters shouted, "Governor, can we have a word with you? There is a lot of news leaking about a military takeover of the federal government. We would like to get the story straight." Jesse smiled and waved as if he didn't hear their remarks, and drove through the gate. Once his SUV was through the gate, members of the Secret Service blocked the road to keep any reporters from following President Hall's vehicle.

Jesse didn't know what kind of plane would deliver him to Washington. He would feel uncomfortable if it was Air Force One. He hadn't yet fully realized that he was the president. The plane turned out to be a small two-engine jet, something a general or high-level cabinet member might use. Jesse thought to himself, *This is more like it.*

The plane landed at 2:30 EST at Andrews Air Force Base, the same airport that Air Force One uses. It was Monday and a normal cloudy day for Washington, DC. Two military vehicles waited for Jesse's plane to stop.

Not much was said. Jesse was hurriedly escorted into the second vehicle, which was running and waiting. Once Jesse was inside, a passenger in the front seat introduced himself. "Sir, I'm Colonel Baker—Roger Baker. I have been assigned to you as your assistant. I will help you get to the many places you will need to be at. I will assist you in doing whatever needs to be done to help with your transition from Texas to Washington, from governor to president. Sir, I am gladly at your service." With that the colonel saluted President Hall. "Sir, I might add that I am from Texas and share your beliefs."

Jesse replied, "Colonel Baker, I'm glad to have you on board. I'm sure we will be spending a lot of time together; I hope I can benefit you in your service to America, and I'm sure you will help me immensely in my service. My first request of you is that in private you call me Jesse and allow me to call you Roger."

Colonel Baker turned a little red and said, "Sir, that will be fine with me. Jesse, our first stop is at the Pentagon; there we will meet with the committee. Every person on the committee is eager to get acquainted with you. Over the last few months, you've expressed the exact views of the committee members. At first we thought Hal Wilson should be installed as president. As time went on, we realized that America is barely hanging on as a country. She has two choices: one to join together as a world government or one-world nation—whatever you want to call this decision. The other choice is for a new, strong government force to take control. Everyone unanimously believed that with Hal Wilson, neither option would work and America would be lost. It seemed like once we had a world government, eventually everyone would end up as a slave in an idealist socialist system. If we take control, it might not work, but there's a chance."

Jesse asked, "Roger, besides this committee, who is behind this movement?"

"I'm glad you asked," Roger said with a lot of excitement in his voice. "The leadership of the FBI, the CIA, thirty-one governors, and all the military, plus some congressmen and a couple of senators. We started this movement nearly two years ago. You may ask why we didn't approach you. The answer is we didn't need to. You were always on our side. You helped us recruit."

Jesse smiled and said, "This is absolutely amazing."

Roger went on to say, "When we arrive at the Pentagon, the plans will be formulated with you as president. We can take over by force, but we hope everyone will join with us. Either way we will take over. No matter how we do it, we will have our opportunity to save America.

"Jesse, there is one problem. We have a constitution and a court system. Although the courts have been improperly used for political gain and the constitution has been set aside many times, what we will be doing is illegal. We will be going against everything legal to save America. We will write our own laws and enforce them. As we do this, many progressive factions will come against us. Not only progressives but people on our side. They have to, to preserve our laws and our future. As you well know, the press will be on the side of the progressives, and eventually so will the uninformed public. Once we set America on its proper foundation, then perhaps we will get a president favorable to our cause. We would hope this president would give us all amnesty. If not, we could spend the rest of our lives in a federal penitentiary.

Chapter 20

The Pentagon

Monday, December 27, 2032

Upon arriving at the Pentagon, the governor's vehicle was directed to an underground parking garage. At the garage the governor's entourage was met with a small security force that ushered them to a meeting room. Once inside, Jesse could see that there were at least fifty people in attendance. Out of respect, everyone stood up and clapped to acknowledge the new president of the United States of America.

After a moment of acknowledgment toward President Hall, Robert Schultz stood up and waved for everybody to take their seats. Colonel Baker directed Jesse to his proper seat. Mr. Schultz went on to say to the people in attendance, "Ladies and gentlemen, I give you President Hall. President Hall, I introduce you to the patriots with whom you will be working to restore America."

Then the chairman of the Joint Chiefs of Staff took his seat as President Hall stood up to speak. "Folks, I don't have much to say, but I wish to thank you for choosing me to be acting president. I'm not sure if I'm the forty-eight or the forty-ninth president. I may not be either of those, but I will serve to the best of my God-given ability to restore America. First, I want to pray for God's hand in our undertaking." With that Jesse prayed, "Father, first I acknowledge You as our only hope to save America. Father, I pray that You would guide each man and woman's heart so that each of us can hear You speak and do what we must do for Your country America. We also confess that as a country You've been set aside. We confess this sin and ask Your forgiveness. I ask You to encourage us in our hearts to set our minds for the task ahead of us and to let us understand that without You, we will fail. Father, thank You for getting us to this place today, and for seeing us through these times ahead. Amen. Folks, I don't know what was planned for today; I suggest that we adjourn and each of us return to our homes and spend time praying and getting prepared for the days ahead. At the same time if you have any reservations, then this will be the appropriate time to turn back. If, when you wake up tomorrow, America's freedom is your cause, then we will meet again and go forward. We may die or be imprisoned, but eventually we will win because God will be leading us."

Colonel Baker stood up as Jesse was taking his seat and said, "Everybody, tomorrow we will meet here at ten o'clock. President Hall will be here for a while to meet as many of you as possible." Before Colonel Baker could introduce anyone to the new president, he leaned toward the president and said, "Sorry, sir, but you need to get acquainted with some of your staff."

Jesse smiled back and said, "Roger, thanks. We're going to do well together."

Ten o'clock came early, and apparently everyone had decided to save America. *It seems as if there are more people in attendance today than yesterday,* thought President Hall as he took his seat. By 10:05 the doors were closed, and Roger stood up to start the meeting. He said, "Well, it looks like we're all here. I'm not surprised. It even looks like we have a few more than yesterday. Before we start, I will ask Secretary Crow to pray." As Neville started to pray, he reached out with both hands, and at once everyone held hands. Then he prayed. Governor Hall noticed everyone holding hands and was encouraged. Until this time he hadn't known where they were spiritually. He thought to himself, *Maybe we just may have a chance—maybe.* Coffee was brought in, and everyone visited for a few minutes before splitting up into different planning groups.

Colonel Baker escorted President Hall to Robert Schultz's office before everyone could sit down. Secretary Crow came into the massive room. Once in the room Robert Schulz, the chairman of the Joint Chiefs of Staff, said, "Men, while we're in this office, let's dispense with formalities and go by each person's first name." He laughed and said, "If everyone called me by my full name, we would be here all night. Jesse, since you are now the president, what are your thoughts on this plan to restore America to what it once was?"

Jesse smiled and said, "I'm glad everyone is sitting down. What I have to say may put a wrench in the plans already laid out. As I explain one view that needs to be considered, please interrupt if you need to inject your thoughts. As it now stands, this Saturday, January 1, 2033, the president will be held at Camp David under house arrest. I will go on national TV and explain what is happening and why. Men, last night I spent most of the night trying to understand any negative consequences that may occur because of our actions. I believe our actions are allowed under the Declaration of Independence. I also believe our opposition will keep us in court for the rest of our lives just to make a point. By the time everyone has had their say, our cause will have been diminished and we will seem like the bad guys.

"Men, this is what I believe should happen. Yes, both President Wiley and Vice President Cunningham should be held at Camp David under house arrest. Then on national TV I will explain to America what these two men nearly did to our country. I will explain about the NATO foreign base commanders being in charge of most of the bases here in America. I will tell them that if we hadn't heard what President Wiley said a few weeks ago, we would have lost America. She would be lost to a small group of evil men, with most of the countries in the world doing exactly the same thing. All the power would be in NATO's hands because they would already have major control of most of the military bases in each of the participating countries.

"I will tell the nation that in the 1960s, America was at work. People had boats, campers, lake houses; they took vacations and ate at nice restaurants. During this time President John F. Kennedy told the American people, "Ask not what your country can do for you but what you can do for your country." That was considered a great speech. Somehow everything is about a great people serving a country. From that point on, the secular progressives gained more power and more power. This was done by making the wealthy America's enemies. Soon prayer was forbidden in schools, and abortion was legalized and became common practice. America was on a downward spiral that couldn't be stopped.

"The government started national health insurance; it stopped most of the energy-producing corporations in America. Welfare was encouraged. After fifteen years or so, America wasn't the same anymore. No work, no boats, no vacations, no cars that could drive across the country. This year, 2032, there is nothing left. This was their plan. They more or less outlawed the wealthy; the tax burden on the middle class became so great that it couldn't be supported by this great nation anymore. They couldn't be defeated until everyone could see how destructive a godless, evil movement that preached equality but passed out slavery really is.

"I would tell America that there might be one more chance for America to be restored. We will have a national election in one month. On the ballot I will be listed as a candidate for president. Vote for me, and if I am elected, America will be restored and returned to the people. I would tell the country that Congress has failed its citizens. If we try to get Congress to act on the many issues we now face, it will only result in continued failure. I will ask for a free hand to turn America around. I have a committee of many great citizens who are dedicated to this great purpose. I ask for four years to accomplish three goals. Number one, have a committee study and do whatever it takes to strengthen the Constitution of the United States of America. Number two, reduce the federal government to the original purpose for which it was founded. Number three, get America back to work. Let the American citizen see what prosperity is really like. Then I would buy a boat and go fishing.

"Gentlemen, those are basically my thoughts. I believe this would kill any hope of future resurrections from the progressives. They will rise again, and it will be our duty to educate the people." Nothing was said; everyone looked to be in deep thought.

Neville began nodding. He said, "Jesse, this is a good plan. I like everything you said. Men, what do you think?" Both Robert and Roger nodded in agreement.

"I would like to add something else," Jesse said. "Upon my winning the presidency, I will initiate term limits. Any bill that I present to Congress will be voted on. If they don't approve the bill, then I will override them. I will do everything I can to persuade them, but what we do to restore America is first on the list. By doing it this way, I won't appear as a dictator."

It was quiet for a minute or so before Roger spoke. "Jesse, yesterday the embassies of Russia, China, and India contacted President Wiley; they demanded an answer for America withdrawing commanders and troops from their countries. They also wanted to know why their commanders and troops were expelled from bases in America. The president has demanded that both Robert and Neville be at the White House this afternoon. We haven't talked to Wiley since his call; he must be very suspicious of our activities. Let's stall him for a few days. There's not much he can do. Let's continue to wait until the first to take over. Both Robert and Neville thought it best to tell the president that the only time both of them will be together is this Saturday or the following Monday. He won't have any choice but to comply.

"Also we will let the president know that after he had his secret meeting December 17, Russia, China, and India had a secret meeting. These countries made a pact between themselves called the Yellow Submarine. President Oner from Russia is a fan of the Beatles, a group from the sixties. Their plan is that immediately after all the nations come together as one unified country, they will be the enforcer of world peace. These three nations will retain fifteen nuclear-powered submarines. Secretly they have built and kept secret the manufacture of Russian K-222 type nuclear-powered submarine. All are very much improved over the previous design. They will be painted yellow and fly their own 'world peace' flag. Their duty will be to go in every port of the unified nations, spending a day or two, showing their power. This is their initial plan, but who knows what's next from these nations. These three countries united several years ago. America fell right in their plans. China and India remained quiet because of our debt and ongoing trade. These subs were tested at night and remained concealed during the day. We suspected they were up to something years ago, but the CIA's ability has diminished over the years, and we were limited in our ability to gather information."

Neville spoke up and said, "Let's do this: send Roger over to see Wiley this afternoon. Roger, tell this idiot president that because of his failed plans and failed leadership, the world is in a mess worse than before World War One or World War Two. Tell him to be quiet and wait until both Robert and I can meet with him. Don't discuss any other details with him. Make sure he knows how displeased we are with him."

President Wiley and Vice President Cunningham were nervously waiting for Roger to be at the White House at two thirty. They had a few minutes to wait and no plans to solve the ongoing issues. As usual the room was filled with strong musty cigar odors and Gerald was sitting slumped in his chair, trying to get a grasp on a desperate situation. Gerald said, "Vernon, all we can do is wait. If there is a coup in progress, we can't respond until we have something to go on. No one from any agency has identified an alert or anything of that nature."

Vernon was chewing on his cigar, trying to understand all the possible situations that could be taking place. He thought about the military withdrawing commanders and troops from foreign NATO bases and expelling foreign commanders and troops from American NATO bases. *Why wasn't I notified?* "Gerald, we've made a lot of secret changes that greatly changed the future of a dead America. Perhaps there are forces operating in secret to try to stop our progress." Before Gerald could respond to President Wiley, the intercom advised them that Colonel Baker was waiting.

As the president's secretary ushered Roger into the room where both the president and vice president were waiting, she introduced their guest. Neither the president nor the vice president stood up to shake his hand. Colonel Baker remained standing. President Wiley said sarcastically, "Mr. Baker, I asked for Neville Crow and Robert Schultz to be here today. What is going on and what do you have to say to me?"

Colonel Baker remained standing, and said, "Mr. President, my name is Colonel Baker; I serve as an officer in the United States Army. I am on the staff of Robert Schultz, chairman of the Joint Chiefs of Staff, who has directed my mission. I am directed to inform you that America is in great peril. The situation we are facing is worse than the one before World War One or World War Two. Mr. President, you had a secret meeting on December seventeenth. At this meeting with the leaders of the seven largest, most powerful nations on earth, you culminated your desire to dissolve America."

President Wiley interrupted him. "Mr. Baker, you don't have to tell me what I know. I want you to tell me what is going on. Do you hear me, Mr. Baker?" President Wiley was obviously very upset and expressed his displeasure by losing his temper.

With firmness of speech, while looking straight into the president's eyes, Roger continued, "Mr. President, with respect to the office of president, I say again, my name is Colonel Baker. I am a colonel in the US Army. I serve on the staff of—"

President Wiley threw his cigar into the trash can and shouted, "Whatever you were sent here to say to me, say to me, Mr. Baker."

Colonel Baker remained standing and said, "Mr. President, my name is Colonel Baker; I serve as an officer in the US Army. I am on the staff of Robert Schultz, chairman of the Joint Chiefs of Staff, who has directed my mission. I am directed to inform you that America is in great peril. The situation we are facing is worse than the one before World War One or World War Two. You had a secret meeting on December seventeenth. At this meeting with the leaders of the seven largest, most powerful nations on earth, you culminated your desire to dissolve America." President Wiley remained silent; he knew to keep his mouth shut. "Mr. President, immediately after this meeting, President Oner of Russia and the presidents of China and India met in private and finalized a plan to inflict terror throughout the world." Roger then explained in detail to both President Wiley and Vice President Cunningham the plans these countries were finalizing. "Mr. President, a few loyal America countrymen in high leadership took the initiative to thwart your evil plans and stop Russia, China, and India from causing catastrophic damage to America and many other countries. It seems to have worked for now. Sir, you have committed an impeachable offense. You will be dealt with in due time. My orders are to recommend that you remain either here or at Camp David until you are told otherwise. This goes for Vice President Cunningham as well.

"Sir, this concludes my message from Chairman Schultz to you. I would like to personally add a comment to you both: America is about its citizens and their God-given freedom, not someone's evil attempt to inflict their own concocted truth. Your self-righteous attempt to create equality, an equality where everyone has less and less as this equality is being distributed—"

Before Roger could finish his words, President Wiley screamed, "We're finished! Get out of my office, now." Roger politely smiled at both of the very rattled men still sitting down, turned around, and left their office.

Chapter 21

Can It Happen? Will It Work?

December 2032

Upon leaving the meeting with both the president and vice president, Roger went back to the Pentagon to report their response to Neville Crow, Robert Schultz, and President Hall. Once in Robert Schultz's office, Roger took his seat and explained how the meeting went. "Men, after I left here, I thought it might be wise to record my meeting with them." As he said this, he took a small recorder from his pocket, and then he played it for the three men awaiting Roger's report. After the recording was finished, Robert said, "Men, I've never been involved in taking over a country, especially my own country. I guess we will have to work through many problems before we can govern as we should. What we're doing is risky business, but I don't see any other way. Do any of you?"

Neville said, "My experience tells me that it doesn't matter how well we make our plans—something unexpected always happens. It always does. I agree with you, Robert, that we don't have much of a choice but to continue and to respond the best way we can."

Jesse then said, "Men, we have three days to think through any scenarios that might pop up. Whatever pops up will more than likely be a severe scenario, one that will challenge our efforts to reclaim America. Let's meet as much as possible and spend the next three days making contingency plans for anything that may go against our plans. I do have a request of each of you gentlemen. We may get arrested and spend the rest of our lives in a federal prison. If this happens, I would like to know more about my partners in crime. I'll go first and share about myself what I think is important and why I'm here."

Jesse shared about his faith in God, his family, and how his father, Orville, had influenced his life. He went on to share that he had planned to go to seminary to become a pastor in a small church somewhere, but that circumstances led him into politics and eventually the office of governor of Texas and perhaps now the president of the United States.

Each man shared from his heart what made him tick. After everyone shared how they got to where they were in life, Roger asked everyone to share some disappointment they had had and how they had handled it. This changed the mood. Roger went first and shared that his family didn't go to church or have any sort of faith in anything. He went on to tell everyone that as a young man he had gotten his fiancée pregnant. They both went to their parents and let them know about the situation. Both sets of parents met and talked and concluded that an abortion would be best for everyone concerned. "I don't think Evelyn really wanted to abort our child," Roger said. "Anyway, she had an abortion. Within a year we broke up. I couldn't get the abortion out of my mind. Later that year a college friend shared Christ with me, and I became a believer. This changed my life. My parents wouldn't let me share Christ with them. They both died without knowing the truth. Evelyn graduated from college, became a schoolteacher, got married, and had two kids. At age thirty-three, Evelyn came down with cancer and died. I don't think she ever got over the abortion. I don't believe she ever went to church. I went to her funeral and visited with her husband. He was an atheist. I went on to West Point and became a career soldier. Shortly after my graduating from West Point, I met and eventually married Glenda, my present and only wife. We have three kids, and as a family, Christ is what keeps us together."

The meeting lasted until late in the evening, and everyone shared. Roger said, "Men, I need to go home before my wife becomes suspicious." Everyone laughed. It was time to call it a night.

On Wednesday everyone met at the Pentagon in a conference room near Chairman Schultz's office. During the brief meeting, Roger held up his hand with four fingers pointing upward, indicating that in four days they would have a new administration in office. Everyone laughed; it was obvious that there was tension in the air. This was a historic event that could go wrong; everyone knew the dangers. Jesse also noticed the tension and was concerned.

Chairman Schultz, Neville Crow, Colonel Baker, and Governor Hall were seated in Robert's office. Jesse waited till everyone finished with their small talk. It seemed as if the conversation last night had had a positive effect on everyone. After a few minutes the chatter died down and everyone looked toward Jesse as if it was his turn to speak. Jesse smiled and said, "It so happens that I do have something to say. I hope we have time for what I'm about to request. I believe it would help our cause if we made a document similar to the Declaration of Independence. Have everyone sign the document. Then have another document that tells in detail what has become of our once great country. Explain that the House and Senate have failed miserably for many, many years, without any hope of correcting what needs to be done for this country to have a chance. Then have a third document explaining what Wiley and Cunningham were trying to do. The fourth document will show what Russia, China, and India were attempting to do. With these documents send a letter saying that as of January 1, 2033, America will have installed a new government. The new leadership asks for America to join hands in a new determination to restore America and go forward with hope. Also it is our desire for this change to be peaceful and orderly. It has taken place and work has already begun. Men, I would like a copy of these documents to be hand delivered to each congressman, senator, and governor, the various secretaries, and cabinet members. Hand deliver these documents at the same time we deal with Wiley and Cunningham. This could be so powerful that many join with us. We will have strong opposition, and they will be afraid to speak against us until they are united against us.

"Concerning the opposition, the progressives aren't as concerned about their many mistakes as they are about staying in power and their ideals going forward. I will go on national TV Saturday and briefly explain what's happening to our country. I will do this often and explain each document in detail; also these documents will be published in newspapers and on the Internet. Well, men, what are your thoughts on what I just said?"

Roger spoke first. "I like it," he said at the same time Robert and Neville said, "I like this plan."

Roger said. "Men, if there is no further discussion on this matter, I need to make arrangements to implement President Hall's plans."

At the White House, President Wiley was meeting with Gerald Cunningham. "Gerald," he said, "I guess you know we're in very serious trouble. I know this is a bad week to have staff meetings and arrange meetings. Gerald, don't you think that we need to go to Camp David tomorrow instead of Friday and try to meet with the attorney general, and members of the Supreme Court—that is, if they will meet with us. You know, the Supreme Court may not meet with us because of their protocol. Also let's talk to the head of the Democratic Party. We will need to have legal counsel, and the party may recommend someone in particular." Gerald didn't say a word. He remained slumped in his seat and Vernon inserted a cigar in his mouth and nervously chomped on it, making a disgusting noise and smell.

It was almost lunchtime, and Robert spoke up, "Men, yesterday I talked to the heads of the FBI, CIA, and the Secret Service. Tomorrow we will meet with each branch separately. Each meeting will be with me or someone on our committee. We have maintained close contact with every person on our list. Everybody will be available to us if we need them. Again, it should go smoothly, but we will have to wait and see."

It was now Thursday afternoon at Camp David, and both Gerald and Vernon were waiting for what they suspected was their demise as president and vice president. Each made several calls in hopes of mounting a defense against the storm that was inevitable. Because it was New Year's weekend, everyone was out of town. The earliest any staff member would be available was Monday, January 3. Sitting in the den with Vernon at Camp David, Gerald spoke first. "Sir, by the time we get a handle on what probably is happening, it will be too late. By then we will have probably died of heart failure. Mmm, that may be the best thing to happen to us, Vernon. What do you think about our situation?" Vernon didn't say a word. He just continued to chew his cigar and look very dismayed.

Chapter 22

One More Chance for America

January 1, 2033

New Year's Day started with sunshine and a clear sky. Colonel Baker thought it was a good sign of things to come. At least he hoped it was.

It was seven o'clock when gate security admitted Colonel Baker onto the grounds of Camp David. A small number of additional Secret Service agents were on duty as a precaution. Close by were army soldiers ready to handle any situation that might arise. High in the sky were army helicopters monitoring anything that might cause concerns.

Both the president and vice president were having coffee in the study; neither was expecting company, but they suddenly saw Mr. Baker walking into the room. Colonel Baker walked close enough to the men that both men could hear everything being said. He stopped and remained standing. Neither the president nor the vice president said a word, and both looked somewhat subdued. "Mr. President, Mr. Vice President," Colonel Baker said, "I come to you today to advise you both that your service as president and vice president has been terminated. As of this moment you both are under house arrest. You will be kept here at Camp David. You will not be able to communicate with anyone on the outside. You will have one assistant; if you need to contact anyone, he will authorize it, if possible."

Vernon Wiley stood up and said, "Sir, do you realize what you're doing to America? Every one of you will be arrested. You won't get away with this."

Colonel Baker didn't reply but remained standing. "Mr. President, that is all I have to say to you." Colonel Baker turned and proceeded to leave the room.

The president said in a loud voice, "What about America? Have you people considered that America could have a national emergency? We could be attacked. This has left America extremely vulnerable."

Colonel Baker stopped abruptly, turned around, and said, "Sir, these are the very reasons these actions have taken place." Without showing any emotion, the colonel turned again, and left the room.

No sooner had Colonel Baker left the study than the Secret Service agents who had been assigned to both the president and vice president entered the room. The senior agent advised both men to turn in any cell phones they might have. He also advised the visibly shaken men that all the phones were disconnected, and then they were introduced to their assistants.

Later that day, America and the world would be notified about the most recent events that had taken place. By then the governors, senators, congressmen, and government officials should have received the documents that had been hand delivered to each of them. Many reporters were stationed at the White House, and many more were at Camp David. It was one thirty in the afternoon, and soon Jesse Hall would address America.

Living arrangements were made for the new acting president at the Jefferson Hotel on Pennsylvania Avenue. From the hotel's conference room President Hall was scheduled to speak to the waiting nation at three o'clock. As the hour approached, the conference room, which could seat five hundred people, filled quickly. The number of reporters was limited to fifty, and no cameras were allowed except for those used by the committee. The other four hundred and fifty seats were filled by a small portion of the many American leaders in support of the movement. There were only two chairs near the podium. Colonel Baker and President Jesse Hall were apparently the only ones to speak at this time. At the back of the room were several Secret Service agents.

Colonel Baker was dressed in a neat gray suit instead of his military uniform. There was a lot of murmuring in the room, but when he went to the podium, all murmuring stopped and there was complete silence. Colonel Baker looked at ease as he began speaking. Jesse knew he was speaking next and was nervous, but as Roger spoke, he became confident and was ready to present himself to America.

Roger started by saying, "Folks, my name is Roger Baker and I would like to introduce the acting president of America to you. Today we have four hundred and fifty great American leaders in this audience. These men and women plus many more have formed a committee to deliver America from its tyrannical leaders. Many of you know Jesse Hall as governor of Texas; he is now acting president of the United States of America." As he said this, he reached out toward Jesse and said, "I give you President Hall."

Jesse quickly approached the podium. Colonel Baker shook Jesse's hand with both of his. As Jesse turned toward the podium, Colonel Baker took his seat. Jesse waited momentarily before speaking. "Ladies and gentlemen, what happened this morning is unprecedented in American history. I hope this never has to happen again. Folks, America has lost her way, and with God's help she may find herself again. Mr. Baker referred to a committee; this committee has been very concerned about losing America to a so-called unified one-world government. That almost happened. Two weeks ago, Vernon Wiley and Gerald Cunningham were making arrangements to do that very thing. They secretly met with the leaders of the seven largest nations to enact their plans—plans to implement a unified one-world government. This was envisioned many years ago. As America declined, this evil force gained power and momentum. It was done by design—cunning, tyrannical design. Once America was combined with other countries, we would lose our identity, our constitution, and our freedom. This was not a concern of these ruthless men.

"While one committee was silently trying to save America, another was trying to give it away. Unbeknownst to Vernon Wiley and Gerald Cunningham, three of the mightiest nations that had joined forces with America to create this new world order, Russia, China, and India, were making separate plans. These plans were to create a secret alliance to gain military dominance over the rest of the world. This was to be done by maintaining large nuclear weapons capabilities. We would surrender all our weapons, including nuclear, while these three countries combined theirs.

"Folks, during the next few weeks this discussion will come up. Many will ask why Congress didn't impeach both Vernon Wiley and Gerald Cunningham. America has a system of laws with which to protect herself. My answer is simply this: anyone in the line to succeed the president and vice president would have led America down the same path it was going. Folks, America as it was founded more than two hundred and fifty years ago has changed. She has changed dramatically from her original concept. We as a nation must decide for ourselves which way we will go. Over the next few weeks, I will share my dream of America being great again. I will ask you to join with me. It's your choice. It's always been your choice. Will you say yes to what our founding fathers started?"

Jesse sat down. As he took his seat, the crowd stood and applauded. He was immediately escorted from the room by Secret Service agents, and the crowd continued to applaud.

Chapter 23

Starting Over

January 2033

President Jesse Hall boarded the military jet early Sunday morning, while it was still dark, headed to Texas. The new president was eager to see his wife and have a long talk with his dad. He knew Clint would be the new governor of Texas instead of joining his staff, but maybe Howard would join him in Washington. Talking to Clint and Howard was another reason for this trip. Jesse needed to be back in Washington by six o'clock Monday evening to speak to America about the ongoing situation. President Hall thought to himself as he boarded the limousine, *Many things to do and not much time.*

It didn't take long for the Secret Service driver to get from Camp Mabry to the Alamo. President Hall slept on the plane, but as he neared his home, he didn't feel very rested. Ellie met Jesse at the door. Not too far behind her was Orville. You could tell both of them had many questions for the new president of America. After kissing Ellie and hugging Orville, Jesse said, "How about a cup of coffee for the president?" Everyone laughed.

It was early Sunday morning, and after coffee and a brief visit, the weary president took a long nap. This was the norm for Sunday. After his nap Jesse wanted to spend time with Ellie and catch up with his dad.

By midafternoon, Jesse was awake and having a ham sandwich with Ellie. "Where are Les and Leigh?" he asked. "I just realized they're not here."

Ellie replied, "Shortly after you left last Monday, Jim, your friend from Fort Worth, came by. He had a friend with him named Chuck. Chuck is a missionary to Mexico, and Jim and Chuck were hauling building materials for an orphanage in Progresso, Mexico. Orville introduced them to Les and Leigh, and we all had Christmas leftovers for dinner together. After visiting a while, Jim offered Les a part-time job in his construction company. He said they could stay in a vacant duplex until they got straightened out. Les shared that he would like to start a new career in gospel music. Chuck said he could help him by introducing him to a few church leaders he knew pretty well. We all passed the hat so they could go back to Ohio and retrieve their belongings and then move to Fort Worth."

Jesse said, "I hope we see them again; they were special."

Jesse spent the afternoon sharing his plans with both Ellie and Orville; he didn't have time to meet with Clint or Howard this time, because he needed to fly back to Washington early Monday morning. Jesse thought it better to leave Ellie back in Texas until his position as president was more solidified, which would take at least a month.

In Washington, early Monday morning came too soon for the new president. His plans for the next thirty days mostly consisted of explaining to the American people his plans and getting their approval so he could follow through. He wanted to get better acquainted with Colonel Baker and try to understand as much as possible about his new duties as president.

At the Jefferson Hotel, President Hall had one floor solely for his use: a large living area as his personal quarters, offices, and a conference room. Jesse didn't think it would be a wise idea to take residence in the White House until he was properly elected. He also thought it best not to use Air Force One until properly elected. The committee had already arranged for a staff of people to help the newly chosen president take charge of America.

While waiting for Jesse, Roger was already in the president's office, instructing the staff about their duties. Once seated in his office with Roger present, Jesse said, "Roger, let's do America right,"

"Yes, sir, I am ready and able," Roger replied with a smile and handshake. "What's on the president's mind today?"

Jesse said, "Roger, I don't think we can legally hold Wiley and Cunningham under house arrest very long. I think we need to free them but not allow them back in the White House or the vice president's quarters. First let's talk to Luis Parton, the attorney general, to see if he will or can file charges on both men."

"Jesse, he has called you several times to speak with you," Roger said.

"Good," Jesse said. "See if he can come over for a visit as soon as possible. If Mr. Parton won't or can't help, contact the US attorney for the District of Columbia; he may help us. The charges will need to eventually be brought up through Congress. Whatever we do, we will be greatly challenged, but it will discredit both Wiley and Cunningham severely in the process. Once we file on them, they're free to leave Camp David. They can stay at Camp David a short time, and then they will have to take care of their own personal living accommodations. Have someone deliver their belongings to them; don't let either Wiley return to the White House or Cunningham return to the vice president's quarters. Also try to get a judge to confiscate both their passports and have them wear ankle monitors."

"Yes sir," replied Roger. "Excuse me momentarily and I will have someone get the attorney general over here for a meeting."

While waiting for a call from Luis Parton, Jesse and Roger visited, and together made hopeful plans for the country. It wasn't until four thirty that the call came in. Mr. Parton could be at the president's office by five thirty. Jesse thought this could be problematic, because he planned to address the nation at six thirty. Roger advised Mr. Parton that their meeting would need to be Tuesday at eleven instead of Monday. While this was taking place, Jesse thought perhaps the attorney general was being difficult with the situation. Roger advised Jesse that Tuesday at eleven wouldn't work for Mr. Parton. Jesse told Roger, "Tell Mr. Parton that he called several times to arrange a meeting with the newly appointed president and to rethink his need to talk with me. If in a few days he still feels it is of some importance to meet with me, then he should call. Let him know upon calling to meet with me that he will need to be available." Roger conveyed the message as told. He reported back to Jesse that the attorney general seemed to be embarrassed and said he would call when he had more time. Upon hearing Roger's last report about the attorney general, Jesse said, "You know, something's a little funny. The attorney general serves at the pleasure of the president. The last president is in jail. I am the new president. Perhaps he needs to get used to his boss being in jail."

Roger then said, "Let's get something to eat before you speak."

This time there was no crowd of supporters in the audience. There were several television crews to film the speech. Jesse was seated at a desk, waiting for six thirty. Before Jesse started his nationwide speech, Roger advised him that thirty-eight governors had signed pledges of support, and eight said they were encouraged and hoped he could turn America around but wouldn't pledge at this time. The other four remained silent, including the governor of Puerto Rico.

The green light came on, and Jesse started his speech. He was relaxed, hoping to instill confidence in America. "Ladies and gentlemen, tonight I will share my plan for America with you. This century is now thirty-three years old. The last time America had a balanced budget was 2001. America has gone downhill ever since. Our great country is sitting on the edge of a cliff. If we don't balance the budget, we will most certainly fall off the cliff. The previous administration's solution for this humongous, catastrophic problem was to unite with all the other countries of the world and combine our resources with theirs. We would have combined our money, which is zero dollars, with theirs, which is also zero. In other words, we would have given away two hundred and fifty years of hard work and what thousands of soldiers have paid with their lives for our freedom. We would trade our history and our future for a piece of bread. That's correct: we would be in bread lines waiting for someone to give us a loaf of bread. We would work many hours and receive two potatoes and a loaf of bread for our pay.

"Folks, that would have been the only possible solution for a failed nation. It would have been the combined result of a failed world economy. If the other countries of the world choose this life or this life is chosen for them, may God help them. This is not the America we want; it was the America a few wicked tyrants hoped for—a nation they could control, as long as they desired, not for you and me as American citizens.

"Mr. Wiley had nearly four thousand people working directly and indirectly for him. Many or most of them didn't report for work, but they received a hefty check. The last few presidents had the same perks. No person or agency cared to confront this issue. This has been going on for years. So if I tell you that I am going to balance the budget, I am going to balance the budget.

"America will thrive again. America is filled with bureaucratic agencies and useless government departments. I'll repeat myself again, if I tell you that I am going to balance the budget, I am going to balance the budget. America will thrive again".

"Our founding forefathers put their lives on the line for America. Many died for our liberty. Today in America, we can't comprehend what real liberty is anymore. Besides balancing the budget, I hope to correct many issues the federal government has failed to deal with. Over the next few days, I will address these issues with you.

"When I was asked by the committee to be president, I said yes, because I still see a glimmer of hope in our country. As we talked about solutions, I realized that America needs a clean slate. The first solution is to stop the bleeding and shrink the federal spending. Allow the American people to prosper. If I went to Congress with my ideas, we all know what the result would be.

"This is my proposal to America. First, the same committee that put me in office can also dismiss me. My reason for telling you this is that our purpose, and only purpose, is to restore America. I don't intend for this to be a dictatorship, and it won't be a dictatorship, but I ask for your total support. My suggestion to the committee was to let the people decide. This February, on Tuesday the eighth, America will have the opportunity to vote for change. I ask for your vote. We took over America, but we can stop if this nation wishes to continue on as before. The ballot will ask, do you want Jesse Hall to be the next president of America? It's either yes or no—you decide.

"If I do become the next president, and I have to persuade the same Congress—the same one that has allowed America to be on the edge of a cliff—it won't and can't work. I need your vote of confidence. I ask for America to give me the power to make the necessary changes we need for success. The ballot will ask, do you give Jesse Hall the power to make the necessary decisions to restore America? Once America is finally restored and we have good and decent people in office, then our laws will again properly govern us.

"Between now and February the eighth, we will talk several times. You as a nation will have plenty of time to make a good decision about America's future. This afternoon I received word that thirty-eight states have joined with us in hopes of a new America. Eight advised us that they are cautious but hopeful. Four didn't reply. I'm grateful for the thirty-eight. I'm sad for the hopeful eight, because this is not a time for cowards to hide. The four are disappointments to the people of their state. They are the very reason America is resting on a cliff.

"Thank you for hearing me share this evening. I ask those who pray to please pray, and those who don't pray to start praying. Thank you, and may God bless America once again."

Roger and Jesse adjourned to Jesse's office. Upon taking their seats, Roger spoke up first. "Good speech, very good. While you were talking, I got a call from Luis Parton. He apologized and said he would be available any time. He said he could be here in fifteen minutes, just to let him know when."

"Great," said Jesse. "Call him now and ask him to come right over."

Roger smiled and said, "Yes, sir."

Then Jesse said, "Roger, I have a staff now. I don't want you to be running errands and answering the phone for me."

Chapter 24

Enormous Challenges

January 2033

Less than fifteen minutes later, Luis Parton arrived at the president's office in the Jefferson Hotel. Jesse sensed that he was a little nervous and greeted him warmly. Roger properly introduced Luis Parton and President Hall to each other, and Jesse shook Luis's hand. Roger said, "Mr. Attorney General, would you like something to drink?"

"No, sir; thanks. I would like for us to get down to business."

Jesse smiled and said, "I like your approach to a difficult situation." The president's office had several upholstered chairs in front of his desk. Jesse and Roger both sat in chairs close to the attorney general. It seemed to create a relaxed atmosphere.

"Sir, since I'm the one who initiated this meeting, please let me speak my mind first. Mr. Hall, you are holding a properly elected president of the United States of America as prisoner. The US Constitution protects our presidents. The elected Congress has the power to impeach him if wrongdoing can be proved. Sir, you have the armed forces, Secret Service, FBI, and CIA supporting this illegal takeover of America. Sir, it won't and must not work.

"I agree that both President Wiley and Vice President Cunningham should be brought before Congress with impeachment charges. That alone must run its on course of justice. The Speaker of the House would be in line to be the next president. This process would allow America, especially in a time of great strife, to continue as a nation of laws. Mr. Hall, if you accomplish this takeover, the result will be disastrous for America. I plead with you to reconsider what you're doing."

President Hall appeared to be calm as he said, "Mr. Parton, we are of many different positions on several issues. I welcome this discussion with you, and I hope that somehow you might see things somewhat differently. First, Speaker Barnes has supported every bill and numerous presidential mandates to turn America over to a unified one-world consortium. As these bills and presidential actions took effect, America wasn't told their real purpose. For example, having our base commanders command overseas bases, and our American bases being run by foreign commanders. This was started several years ago; it was Speaker Barnes who introduced this bill in Congress. It was introduced as a military unification effort. This was sold to America as a method of keeping the United Nations forces ready in any part of the world as one mighty force.

"Speaker Barnes is the force behind Vernon Wiley. Also the approval rating of Congress is less than five percent. This is lower than the eight percent it's been for the last twenty or so years. Mr. Parton, America had no leadership in place to properly execute needed change. The fact is that the seven largest countries and America needed to unite just to continue operations. Once this happens, the rest of the G22 nations would be forced to comply.

Mr. Parton, can you begin to understand the results for this nation once this does happen? These plans were being made with several past presidents with the continued leadership of Speaker Barnes. Mr. Parton, most nations are just like America: they also are at the edge of a cliff, about to fall into some kind of abyss. We have only one chance left. It is to separate ourselves from this unified world destruction and somehow start over. America first—the people, not the government. This can't be done unless we start over completely. As you can see, my first plea is for the people to support me, and then the governors. This should force Congress to follow suit. Mr. Parton, this isn't a takeover; this is an attempt to steal America from tyrants and return it to the rightful owners. Luis, I personally invite you to be a part of American history. You must decide how you will be remembered. You must be strong enough to pay whatever the cost may be. Go home and consider what was said, think about what is right, and then call me. I will be waiting for your call."

With that last remark Jesse stood up to escort the attorney general to the door. Mr. Parton looked to be in deep thought as he walked to the door. He shook hands with Jesse, nodded, and then left.

Chapter 25

Getting Through January

January 4, 2033

It was early Tuesday, January 4, when Attorney General Luis Parton called President Hall. He called to offer his services in any capacity to the new administration. They met for lunch and planned for Luis to have Congress bring impeachment charges against both Wiley and Cunningham. They agreed to further investigate to find out who might be involved in the plot to terminate America as an independent nation. Roger shared that the FBI had been active in gathering information about several national leaders who were deeply involved in this conspiracy; many were serving in Congress. Both Luis and Jesse were surprised to find out about the country's national leaders. For now, Luis thought that both the president and vise President shouldn't be confined and held. They would have forty-five days to obtain personal living quarters, or they could stay in a military installation near Washington; it would be their choice. Once the news hit the media, the remaining eight states expressed a strong desire to join forces with the newly established American government. The other two states, New York and California, had always supported extreme liberal causes; so far they continued to reject the new administration.

The committee that installed Jesse Hall as president wasn't idly standing by; many plans were being made to reestablish America as it once was. One committee was in charge of rewording the Constitution.

The original wording allowed slavery to continue and denied women their voting rights. The point at which a person was considered a viable human being had never been defined. The Thirteenth and Nineteenth Amendments made changes as far as slavery and giving voting rights to everyone, but perhaps this was the time to include complete equal rights for every person from conception to grave.

While a new set of rules were secretly being written to strengthen the Constitution and prevent abuses from every branch of the federal government, President Hall was very active in strengthening his position as president. Jesse now had the unanimous support of forty-eight states. The polls showed an 88 percent favorable rating, even in New York, and in California the favorable rating was slightly over 65 percent, causing great consternation for the governors of both states.

The sitting Congress was extremely subdued by the recent actions of a few determined men in very high places. Most of the members of Congress knew America was inches from falling off the cliff. Although they knew this very well, most of these individuals weren't actively supporting the new president.

Roger, the trusted aide of America's new president, still didn't have a job description or a title. He could be the chief of staff or maybe even the vice president. Jesse didn't take time to sort this out; the many tasks in front of both men were their greatest concerns. After the vote this matter would be settled.

It was now Wednesday, January 26, and much had been accomplished, but Congress was still very much alienated from the new committee-appointed president. The temporary office of the president was humorously called the Rectangular Room. Here in the rectangular room sat Roger, Luis, and Jesse. Roger spoke first. "Men, it is time to win over Congress. I have the list of the congressmen and senators who are very much involved in plotting with Wiley and Cunningham to overthrow America. Yesterday, I met with the FBI and they shared some very interesting documents with me. This has been planned for several years. The proof is overwhelming. There are forty-nine congressmen and eight senators. The governor of New York also actively participated in many of their secret meetings. I suggest we offer amnesty to each of these men. This amnesty means only that they immediately resign from office. If they don't, they will be prosecuted with Wiley and Cunningham. It would be a pleasure to bring disgrace to these men, but right now we need to have Congress on our side. I will add that part of the amnesty deal is that these men won't be prosecuted in a federal court. Each state can do as it wants with them. Most of them were untouchable until we took over, but now they're not so untouchable.

"Also, each of these men is very wealthy. Over many years large sums of money have been deposited to a secret foreign account, from a secret fund. Luis will send each one a letter saying that it is of utmost importance that they attend a meeting held in our conference room. Once in the meeting they will each receive a packet of documents showing their involvement in treason against America. They will have twenty-four hours in which to resign. Each person must sign a document acknowledging their guilt and saying that they will never seek public office again. Upon their immediate retirement the illegal funds will be frozen and none of these men will receive a pension from the federal government.

"Although this will help with a few congressmen and senators, we still will need to win over those who remain. I suggest that we enlist the governors of every state to help us. Each of us and several of the supporting congressmen and senators will personally visit each governor and persuade the governor to convince their congressmen and senators to offer their complete support for our cause. We will explain to each governor that it is of great necessity that we have a majority of the American people, the governors, and Congress on our side.

"So far the press hasn't hurt our effort, but they will go negative if it will help them sell more newspapers. If we have everyone on our side, we can turn America around. Also the governors will need to express to their senators and congressmen that both bodies need to give this administration a vote of confidence. Once we have Congress on our side, the press will be somewhat muted. As we began to really make changes, we will need to maintain as much support as possible. It will be very difficult; we will have to keep the governors involved. Once the changes are made and in force, the states will benefit the most, which should encourage the governors to continue to help us."

As the month went by President Hall spoke to the nation many times. Each time he explained his plan in great detail. As this was being done, the nation seemed to regain hope.

Chapter 26

Referendum

February 8, 2033

By January 31, all the congressmen and senators implicated in the "throw America under the bus" scandal had resigned. The press managed to report this story in the greatest of detail. As each retired, disgraced politician arrived in their home state, a large crowd of people greeted them to personally express that they were no longer welcome there.

The same news quickly spread to New York, where the people demanded that the governor vacate his office. Although the governor of California wasn't implicated, his views about the new administration caused thousands of protesters to be at every function he went to, demanding his immediate resignation.

Jesse was amazed. In one month America had awakened. He had support from probably 90 percent of the people, the governors, and many of the congressmen and senators. One problem hung heavily on Jesse's newly formed government. Many congressional leaders and members were using the rule of law to go against Jesse's new government. They said that what the new administration was attempting to do was commendable but illegal. The established laws were in place and working, they said, and were designed to protect the people and maintain law and order. Those laws must be observed at all cost.

It was now Saturday, three days before America was to decide what leadership would guide the country. It was obvious that President Jesse Hall would win the national election. Jesse knew that if he didn't have a mandate from the people, the governors, and the legislative branch of the federal government, it would be for naught. He knew if he dissolved the EPA by presidential mandate, Congress would override his decision. He could force his mandates, but if he did, his actions and presidency would be short lived and ineffective. It would be the same as it had been for many, many years.

By now the committee was several thousand strong. Each state had several hundred respected leaders serving in leadership positions on the committee. Jesse's brain trust, which consisted of Jesse and Roger, thought it was time to try to force the hand of the legislative branch. Jesse again reached out to the American people. In Sunday's broadcast from the Jefferson Hotel, President Hall exclaimed, "Dear American citizens, in two days you will vote to give me a mandate to take back America. What each of you will be doing is giving me permission to get America back on her feet. I need each of you, each and every person listening to my voice, to get involved. Your involvement is crucial for the success of America. Starting today the many news outlets will publish the names of all the American citizens who are serving on the committee. There are thousands. Most states have well over a hundred committed Americans dedicated to change.

"Folks, I remind you, nothing's changed. We are still on the verge of government collapse. I would like for you to see the men who gave me this daunting job as president. They can also remove me from office if the need arises. America is in a time of desperate measures. We all need to get very involved. The federal government has failed you as American citizens. This fledging administration has the support of forty-eight governors and ninety-one percent of the American citizens. Still, Congress continues to be a stumbling block. Starting right now, call your congressmen and senators, and demand that they support this administration. For years the legislative branch has failed to act to preserve our way of life. Now they claim to be the only way America will survive. As each congressman and senator continues to resist restoring America to its previous greatness, you will be notified daily from the many news outlets. Please visit their offices and their homes, and demand that they support the new, temporary government. Each congressman and senator must pledge complete support for America to be reestablished and be a vibrant nation again.

"During this time of great change, I will make the decisions I believe are best for America. There isn't time to present bills to Congress for debate. There isn't time for failure as it was in the past, failure that we citizens paid dearly for several times over, failure for their poor judgment and bad decisions. I will make whatever decision is best for the individual citizens. My policies will not be based on the good of the country or the common good of the people. My decisions will be based on what should be done to allow a person to have liberty and freedom and to get the government out of their lives. Every person has the right to prosper and continue to thrive as an America citizen.

"Folks, it does matter what each of you do as citizens. If you fail, America fails. If you are successful, then America has a future. Now it's your turn. Go vote Tuesday, but tomorrow visit your congressmen and your senators, and tell them you want America back."

At the Jefferson Hotel on Sunday evening, several committee leaders, known and respected nationally, were on hand to make a national pitch for President Hall. The country was told in an encouraging way that America would rise again and be as great as before. One nationally recognized American leader tried to explain that it was beyond him and most Americans as to how the United States had ended up on the brink of national oblivion. We all watched Europe go down the tube, and somehow we had done exactly the same thing, he said. How did this happen? After making a passionate speech, he said, "However, whatever caused America to be blind and stupid for such a long time must be addressed. We must never follow the same paths again."

On Monday night President Hall again spoke to the nation. He explained that many congressional and senatorial leaders were coming around. He explained why he must have the people, the governors, and Congress on the same side. President Hall went on to say that being a Democrat or a Republican was a good thing, but that it was much different now. It was about America only, not any one political party. America first, political parties later, he said.

By seven thirty eastern time, most of the votes were in. The results were enough for the new president to say that he was now the people's choice. Less than 1 percent had voted to leave the country as it was. President Hall had a clear mandate from the people, and he would use it to sway the few remaining senators and congressmen to join with the people of America for a chance to live as Americans should be able to live.

At nine o'clock eastern time, President Hall addressed the nation. He thanked everyone and said it was almost time to go to work. A few senators and congressmen were resisting, but he had confidence that soon everyone would participate in a renewed America.

Chapter 27

Almost There

Tuesday, February 8, 2033

Almost there wasn't the same as being there. In the Rectangular Room of the Jefferson Hotel were the newly elected president, Roger, and several staff members from the committee. Roger spoke first. "All of you know your assignments. It is extremely important that each of you succeed. In the next two days someone from your team will have talked directly to the governor about a congressman or a senator who is resisting the people they represent. We need to have the governor exert as much pressure as possible on anyone who is holding back support. At the same time some of your team members will be working the press. Your assignment is to personally contact the senator or congressman you have been assigned. We will have made contact with them, so they will be expecting you. Each of you has been briefed about your best approach to the person you will be seeing. If everything you try fails, then it will be time to share that the people and leadership in their state will soon be asking for a recall vote. Tell your person you can't make a deal; all you can do is receive their total support. Wait a minute and then politely leave." As each person left, President Hall and Roger Baker stood at the door to shake their hand and personally thank them for their dedication.

February was warmer than usual, and by the fifteenth, most of the senators and congressmen had committed to join with the citizens and the governors in support of the new American president. As Roger was having great success with his get-out-the-support campaign, the president was working on the next and final phase of what he thought was needed to begin his work.

It was now Tuesday, February 22, and President Hall was eager to start his work on restoring America. At four thirty in the conference room, assembled and waiting were most of the forty-nine House members and six of the senators, who just one month ago had been discharged and left Washington humiliated and disgraced. No one really liked what had happened to them or who had caused it. President Hall hoped to give them a chance for redemption.

"Men," said the president, "I know what each of you must be going through at this moment. I also know that last month was probably the worst month in your life. When you arrived at your homes, the American people met you and shamed you. Now it's only a few days later and you've been asked to return to Washington. You weren't told why you were needed in Washington, only that it was very important that each of you come to this meeting.

"Folks, each of you knows about gridlock, political pettiness, whatever you wish to call our political process in America. America can't continue if drastic changes aren't made immediately—needed emergency changes to help the people get going again, not some bureaucratic entity that will grow and swell and always be ineffective. You know there is a great majority of the population behind what we're doing, plus forty-eight governors, and many senators and congressmen. This is what I need from you. I need your support. You left in shame. If each of you address Congress and encourage them to pass a bill that will be introduced—a bill giving me the needed power to do what must to be done for the sake of the American people—then each of you will be able to return to your state with your head held high. You will have put your name in history as heroes. This heroic action will right many wrongs; men, please don't pass this opportunity by. I'm going to ask all in support of this offer to stand. If you're not in support, please leave the room." Nothing happened for a moment. The men muttered between themselves. They knew they had only one choice. Everyone stood up. They didn't smile, but they stood up.

Roger said, "Men, we have arranged for accommodations for you. There are attendants waiting to help you with your stay and your activities while you are here. My name is Roger Baker, and your aide will give each of you my card. If you need me for anything, please call."

An emergency bill that would give the newly elected president unprecedented complete power over the federal government would be presented to Congress later that week. It would come up for a vote by the end of the next week. The returning disgraced congressmen met privately with many of the serving members of the House and Senate. Some went on the news channels to explain what must be done and why.

President Hall felt pretty good about the outcome of the vote. He knew it could go either way but thought surely it must go his way. The date for Congress to vote was set for Friday, March 4. Congress was called to order, and the acting Speaker introduced the bill to the members for a vote. He said, "I would like your attention, please. Past Speaker Barnes of the House has asked permission to speak. I have no objections. He will speak. Mr. Speaker, you have the floor."

The fellow disbarred senators and congressmen who had joined with the president were in attendance in the visitors' gallery. Ex-Speaker Barnes would join them there after his speech.

The press gallery was filled with reporters. Ex Speaker Barnes stood in front of the podium as he had done for years. Mr. Barnes was a short man with thick glasses. As he started speaking, he removed his glasses to wipe tears from his eyes. "America, I'm sorry. Fellow congressmen, I'm sorry. I brought shame to this body. I will spend the rest of my days trying to earn your respect again. I was trusted with the affairs of this great nation. I failed miserably. Because of men like me, America is at a crossroads. One road is short and is a dead end. We don't know what the outcome will be if that road is taken, but we know it will be very bad. The other is a long road that is scary and fraught with many challenges. This is the only road we can take.

"Our past history shows us that we wouldn't take either road. We avoided the fix and wouldn't acknowledge our failure. Now by God's providential care we may have another chance to go down the right road together. Our issues are great, and we must have a drastic change for this nation to set her course on the only road that will lead us to where we should be. Men and ladies of this Congress, you have only one way to vote. I trust today marks the beginning of what America should be. May God bless America again." With that Speaker Barnes left for the gallery, where his fellow congressmen and a few senators waited and clapped. Everyone stood up and clapped until he left the large auditorium.

Chapter 28

Final Vote

Friday, March 4, 2033

By now both the House and Senate had voted. It was a landslide. Of the active 288 congressional members, 270 had voted for the Emergency Powers Act, giving President Hall unprecedented powers as president. The Senate voted earlier the next day, a Saturday, and it was another landslide. Of the ninety-two active senators, seventy-eight voted yes. It was now time for Jesse Hall to do his duty as president.

It was now four in the afternoon on Friday, March 4. President Hall was speaking to Ellie on the phone and telling her she would be moving to the White House next week. Ellie, a little nervous, said, "Honey, I can't wait to be with you in the White House, but I really hate for us to be so far from Mom, Becky, and your dad. Do you think I can spend three or four days a month back here? It sure would make me feel better about being the first lady. What do you think about that, Jesse? Excuse me, I meant to say 'Mr. President.'"

They both laughed, and Jesse said, "That problem can be solved easily enough. I wish the others were that easy to solve. Anyway, honey, I need to go. I'll call you tonight when I get finished. Love you. Bye."

Jesse then turned to Roger. "Roger, this is what I'm thinking right now. I want to meet with Willie Barnes about being my chief of staff. I like how he helped us win over Congress. Also, I would like you to be the vice president, but not in the conventional way. In the past the vice president was a mostly ceremonial position. What I need from you is for you to continue just like you're doing. Roger, I don't think we would have been as successful if you hadn't been here.

"Also I want to keep Luis as attorney general. You remember Howard, Texas's attorney general. I will ask him to join with several others to review the Constitution. The first item is—are you ready for this?" Jesse smiled and said, "The first thing I plan to do is move the United Nations out of New York and sever our relationship with the UN. I'm also going to sever our relationship with the G22 Conference. All foreign aid will stop and be reviewed—our support of South Korea, for instance. We spend untold billions on their defense, whereas they spend very little, and then we buy ninety percent of their exports—just to support their economy. This must change. In some countries we give the president, or whatever title he goes by, millions of dollars just to let us defend his country. I would like to meet with both Robert and Neville as soon as possible to discuss these topics.

"I understand our soldiers are all back home from serving in the UN at various places throughout the world. Also I would like to use the army to secure the borders around this country. We have a small, ineffective Border Patrol. We will phase them out and use the army. Also we'll use drones to identify anything coming across the border and to identify dope-smuggling submarines. My thoughts are that once a dope-smuggling submarine is identified as such, then blow it out of the water.

"Actually, Mr. Vice President, would you meet with Robert and Neville by yourself? Then we can decide later how to approach this. Next on the agenda is balancing the budget. Some of the recent ex-House and ex-Senate members were on different finance committees. I would like to have a couple of economists, and together they will work as a committee. They will go over every department and agency that is funded by the federal government. For example, Planned Parenthood receives millions from the federal government. The national government has created thousands of jobs by creating agencies, bureaus, secretaries, and assistant secretaries. The Constitution didn't allow for a burdensome, bloated government. What we need to find out is what is actually needed for the safety and protection of the American citizen, and we need to know if this is really the responsibility of the federal government. As soon as we have the necessary information on each entity, we will immediately cancel its operations if it's not needed. Between the president and vice president there were more than five thousand employees. Many senators and representatives have as many as three hundred workers serving them, each with a budget of four or five million dollars annually. This must be stopped, and somehow the Constitution must prevent it from ever happening again."

Roger smiled, and said, "Is that all?"

Jesse laughed and replied, "No, probably not. I will probably think of something else long before Monday. Well, actually, one of the next items to explore is the EPA. Their vast powers will be limited, and their funds will be cut drastically. Along with that, cancel the restrictions on drilling for oil and the restrictions on coal-fired power plants. Lastly see about federally assisted bank loans for small business and farms. Okay, that's all. Go try to have a nice weekend, and thanks for being the vice president."

Roger smiled and said, "Thank you, sir. This was much faster than going up through the ranks."

Chapter 29

Happy Days Are Here Again

President Hall's administration was in place, and changes were on the way. The people were anticipating great things for America; excitement was in the air, although nothing had happened yet. Maybe it was that some of the news stations were playing "Happy Days Are Here Again" before each news broadcast. In past years the press had vehemently opposed any conservative approach to governing. The opposition was usually indirect but nevertheless very effective.

Howard was now working in the White House, trying to organize the best way to make needed changes in the Constitution. In their daily meetings it was decided that Speaker Barnes would engineer a plan to effectively present each amendment separately to congress and then to the states for approval. Once each new amendment was approved, the next one would be sent for congressional action. The committee had many people working in each state to influence the congressional members and the senators, but everyone knew it would be an uphill battle to change the Constitution.

The first constitutional change was to be an amendment about declaring America a Christian nation. Much had been said about protecting one's right to worship as one chose, and that protection would remain. Great detail went into explaining that not much was written about our forefathers being Christians. Many were believed to be Deists, which is certainly not Christian. Many details were written about America's founding fathers but not so much about their Christian faith.

The Christian Acknowledgment Amendment gave freedom to the many who didn't believe, but it wanted to acknowledge God above all. As Howard's staff met with various congressmen, they used Psalm 33:12 to express their beliefs: "Blessed is the nation whose God is the Lord; and the people whom he hath chosen for his own inheritance." The staff members often said that the destruction that was upon the nations of the world was directly caused by each nation turning away from God. People's only chance to survive, they said, was to acknowledge God and, for the ones who did believe, to pray for his blessing on America.

Many liked the concept of separation of church and state, or freedom from religion, and having a nation where God was neutral in the land except by each person's separate and private choice. Howard's staff amply defined that the nation had basically two kinds of people: ones who did believe, with different amounts of understanding and many different kinds of churches, and the ones who don't believe—they just didn't. Over many, many years the latter had somehow excluded God from America. They had won the argument because there was no argument. The plain fact was that God was not welcomed in America. If people wanted America to destroy itself, then they should continue to deny God. He was their only chance for survival as both individuals and as a nation. That was the message Howard planned to use to reach America with hopes of amending the Constitution to acknowledge God as Lord, benefactor, and Savior.

It was Friday, March 11, and President Hall had planned a quiet weekend with First Lady Ellie Hall. As Friday wore on, he knew it was time to enact many drastic changes. As he walked from his office to his living quarters, he knew he would be very preoccupied with the many much-needed changes ahead of him. Jesse thought, *Tonight we will have a nice dinner and then watch a movie, but tomorrow we must decide what to do and do it.* Jesse turned around and went into his office just in time to catch Juanita Salazar, his personal secretary, who was about to leave. "Juanita, I hate to interrupt your weekend, but we need to have a staff meeting tomorrow. Please have someone make the necessary calls. I will need someone here to take notes for later discussion and reference."

Juanita didn't smile, nor did she frown. She said the usual, "Yes, sir, I will take care of it right away. Is that all, President Hall?"

Jesse replied, "Yes, Juanita, that is all. I can't thank you enough."

Juanita smiled and said, "Good night, sir."

Ellie knew Jesse was preoccupied, but the dinner was great, and they enjoyed the movie. Not much was said. Jesse was mulling over the many actions that would be announced to his staff the next day. Ellie knew Jesse was trying to make sure nothing would be left to chance, and let the evening be a quite one.

Chapter 30

The President Goes to Work

The meeting was set for ten in the morning in the Situation Room of the White House. Vice President Baker came early to go over the topics to be discussed. They had a light breakfast and were prepared for the meeting. By ten o'clock, everybody was seated and quiet and ready for the meeting to start.

Vice President Baker opened with a short prayer and then began his explanation to the staff. "Folks, each of you knows full well what needs to be done for America to have a chance at recovery. Now, recovery in the previous sense of the word meant something to be obtained. That's not the case today. If we don't have a recovery, we don't have an America—it's that simple. The government has expanded and expanded without any financial resources to pay for expansions.

"Shortly President Hall will detail his immediate plans to stabilize America. Before the committee selected President Hall, lengthy studies were done to determine how to go about reclaiming America. It was originally supposed to be 'of the people, by the people, and for the people,' but today it is 'of the government, by the government, and for the government.' If the people don't support this plan, it won't and can't work.

"Miraculously the press has supported everything that we've done, but we haven't changed the government yet. We expect the press to turn against us with both barrels when this happens. As soon as these changes are implemented, we will have a war of words and ideas.

"Many still believe secular humanism and extreme liberalism is the way of the world and the world's only future. The horrific past decades haven't changed their minds. This is their religion, and they have dying faith in their religion. Our problem with their religion is that we will all die. We must communicate truth to the millions of Americans who still don't understand how and why we got this way. The millions were told they would receive help from the government, and millions are still waiting for better days. Yes, sadly, millions are still hoping for America to come through. She can't and won't.

"There is one thing in our favor that we didn't plan for. For many decades the federal government has had very low ratings with the people, as have both political parties. What's very unusual and unexpected is that the committee and President Hall are not associated with any of these groups. As we connect to the people, we will promote constitutional government, going back to a neighborhood church, working for a living—in other words, a new life, like it was originally meant to be in America. President Hall, what is your plan, sir?"

President Hall looked over everyone and, keeping his seat, said, "Thank you, Vice President Baker. As the vice president just shared, much discussion and planning has already been done on the necessary and immediate changes in America. This is only the first round. As we gain strength, we will make many more changes. Our strength will be determined by whether or not the people join us. If they don't support us, we fail, and America fails. So really, saving America is not about us sitting here making decisions. It is about America being hungry for truth and change.

"The first changes will be cancelling our membership and support of the United Nations. The offices in New York will be closed. We will also cancel our membership in and support of the G22 Conference. Many of our embassies will be closed throughout the world. Where we have an ally, we will maintain an embassy, but with a reduced staff. These changes could cause great problems throughout the world. As each of you know, for years we've made our enemies rich just by them hating us. We operated in fear and let evil rule. It is time for a vastly different approach. Just a few months ago, our allies Russia, China, and India conspired against us to gain political world power. Every country in the world has the same problems we do. What we are doing could cause a war. We hope and pray that it doesn't. Nevertheless we must act alone and decisively.

"Another change is that no foreign power, organization, or person can own any part of America—property, stock, or debt. America will assume any of these situations from their source. Then we will negotiate a settlement with whatever foreign entity has a stake in America. If any American citizen owns property, stock, or debt in a foreign country, that will be their issue, and America will not be involved.

"The United States of America will not own property throughout America. All properties owned by the federal government will be sold at a low interest rate to whatever state the property is in. This does not apply to military installations.

"The next item is going to a flat tax system. The tax rate will be a flat rate of 15% for everyone who works, with no deductions. If a person willfully cheats on their taxes, they can be convicted of a felony. This change will mean an immediate eighty-five percent personnel reduction at the IRS.

"Remember the stimulus plans that were used by different administrations several years ago? They didn't work very well at all. We're hoping the flat tax plan does really work and that the country's revenues vastly increase. If that happens, that means recovery is happening and those entitlements can be funded with revenue instead of creating unpaid debt. Then America will properly be financially managed.

"Next on the agenda is the federal budget. It will be called a pie. Often a pie is used to illustrate how funds are being distributed, but each slice is always changing size. Once each slice is allocated, it will be implemented and not changed. It for some reason we have a national emergency, we will assist each state as best we can, but the money will come from another piece of pie, not from creating debt.

"We've tried to look at the entitlements to see what is really needed. This was impossible. There are many agencies designed to help with a cause or a national need, but for forty-five years or more, we've had no money to fund them. Do you know that for years there were no benefits paid out? Still these agencies grew and continued to be a very large federal drain. In the first federal budget of this administration, only ten percent will be allocated for benevolence. These funds will be distributed by each state and will be apportioned according to their population. Each state decides where to spend their portion of the pie.

"Social Security is a mess. For every person receiving Social Security, only two-point-seven people are contributing. We will start with a federally independent consortium that will invest the employees' Social Security taxes. It will start with the people who will retire in fifteen years. As you all know, the employer matches the employee's contribution. This will now go toward the participants already receiving Social Security benefits. Also a surtax of ten percent will be charged to the consortium from each person's deposit, which will also be used for the participants already on Social Security. Once the number of retired people on the old system is reduced, these funds will go toward Social Security Disability Insurance and Medicare benefits. Our plan is to eventually get the government out of Social Security and federally sponsored insurance. It has always been known that private industry can do a better job than the federal government. This is a piece of the pie that will be a burden for everyone for a few more years.

"Today America is giving colleges and universities millions and millions of dollars to teach our kids to hate America and that secular humanism is the only way to truth. As of right now, no college or university will receive any more federal funds. Their slice of pie is not from the federal government.

"The Supreme Court and all federal judges will now have some accountability. Their duty will be defined as interpreting the law as it was written, not writing or changing the law as they determine. A few months ago the Supreme Court allowed Vernon Wiley and Gerald Cunningham another term. In their ruling they said it was 'best for

America at this time.' There will be a federal prosecutor and grand jury convened at all times to properly deal with activist judges. Any improper action from a sitting judge will be cause for his or her removal from the bench. I might add that the first duty of the new appointed prosecutor will bring integrity to the Supreme Court.

"Term limits: as of right now, all members of the House will be able to serve only two terms of three years each. Senators can serve one term of six years. They will still be entitled to their regular pay, but there will be no retirement benefits for either group.

"Besides the vocal, politically active news media, lobbyists appear to make up a silent secret arm of the legislative branch of the government. I don't have time to explain in detail the new rules for lobbyists, but I will say this: as of today, their influence is greatly if not totally diminished.

"There are three branches of government; there are also three kinds of insurance. The most favored government employees have an excellent plan. The majority of citizens are under the Affordable Health Care Act, which is not affordable and does not provide much health care. Medicare has become very expensive, and the coverage is limited. A veteran has to wait for months to see a doctor or practitioner. Government-managed health care has killed more people that the worst diseases. The deluxe plan offered to the elite only will still be offered, but now the elites will have to pay the difference for the so called deluxe health benefits. Everyone will have the same insurance coverage. The committee has researched health care in depth. It seems as if what we're paying, and what we're ending up with, is an indirect federal tax that leaves citizens with very expensive marginal coverage. Again the solution is a simple one. The federal government needs to get out of the health care business and the insurance business. We're hoping that this boondoggle can be corrected within two months.

"As America makes these important and necessary changes, many will soon see new opportunities for starting a business or expanding a business that's been hanging on for years. Some businesses have closed but may reopen. We will be standing by to help. We will lend states money to energize the economy. Some states have a sales tax, a property tax, and a state income tax. If the federal government is reducing its burden on each citizen but states increase their burdens on citizens, then we're not going anywhere. Our rate of interest will be proportioned to how much a state taxes its citizens. At the same time the rate each citizen has to pay in interest will be the same for every state.

"We know that America will be isolated from the world, except for a few allies who have always been friends. Eventually they will get over their anger. The worst problem facing humanity on this planet is hunger and water. Our greatest asset is producing food. No country can match us. We plan to open more farmland, and we hope many people return to the farm like their fathers and mothers. That will help stabilize the world and America.

"The border problem has never been resolved. The US Army will now have the responsibility of securing both the north and south borders. Measures will be taken to apprehend all illegal aliens and expel them permanently from American soil. An employer who hires an alien will be charged with a felony, and the punishment will include a stiff fine. Once our economy has sustained growth, we will devise a method that offers work permits. Any person working must have a permit and will be required to pay taxes like everyone else.

"I must tell each of you that these changes will have a great effect on every citizen in America. Many will love us and many more will hate us, but we must act. The great political leaders of both parties somehow used sleight of hand or some other magical method to transfer the wealth of a nation from the people to the government. As regulation after regulation burdened the small-business man and large corporations, they began to close. Very few companies could afford the Affordable Family Health Care Act. It was the final tax that closed the door on both the wealthy and the middle class. As the number of very successful people shrank, so did the middle class. The working class grew by leaps and bounds, but sadly we had no jobs for these American citizens to do. These are the methods of a progressive form of government. The problem is that very few people understand what happened and why. Here in my hand is a folder of information about agencies, staffs, committees, and government organizations that employee thousands upon thousands of federal employees. Their benefits are much better than those of equal position in the regular workforce. Most of these people got their job because they know somebody, and many aren't qualified to do their very costly bureaucratic jobs.

"This concludes our first session. We will see change. Tomorrow Speaker Barnes, Vice President Baker, members of my staff, and I will begin to implement some of the changes that must take place. They won't be easy, but eventually America will be able to smile again."

Vice President Baker stood up to dismiss the meeting. "Thanks, folks. Your dedication is very much appreciated. Soon we will see the fruits of your dedication. God bless each of you. You are dismissed."

As almost everyone left the room, Speaker Barnes remained behind. He walked over to where the president and vice president were having a conversation. "Mr. President, may I have a word with you, sir?"

Jesse said, "Sure. Let's all go to my office and have a talk."

Once they were in the office and sitting down, Willie Barnes appeared somewhat stressed and began to explain. "Mr. President, Mr. Vice President, tomorrow when I present these mandates to the sitting Congress, we will have a wave of fired congressmen and congresswomen after our hides. Please, let me suggest what I see as the best way to implement these changes you just proposed. First implement term limits, as of right now. Let the retiring legislators serve out their term in congress. Have the governors from the different states that are affected immediately appoint new legislators.

"During this period of time we will be able to prioritize our agenda. We will institute specific time limits for each bill in committee. That will give us time to deal with laws to limit the activities of the lobbyists." Speaker Barnes then looked directly at President Hall and said, "Sir, no one knows how Congress will take to your changes. Only time will tell. It may be good or it could be bad for the constitutional changes you hope to have.

"My personal thoughts are what history has told us. Constitutional changes are always very hard to get passed. Again, I suggest first trying what you believe are the most important changes to the Constitution. As this administration clamps down on America, your popularity will diminish. Strike while you're loved, not after. We have powerful groups in every state that can influence the vote. Let them loose, let them win America over while they can. Once we have our way, then we will work on the many other items that need to be changed." With a slight smile Speaker Barnes said, "That's all I've got."

Roger said, "Thanks, Willie. This will give each of us something to think about and a place to start tomorrow."

Chapter 31

Get 'Er Done

Monday, March 14, 2033

What to do next was already decided, but making changes was taking longer than what President Hall had hoped for. Shrinking the federal government and reducing the federal debt to a manageable level was an impossibility in most politicians' minds. It was never a reality. President Jesse Hall was eager to get started, but just getting started seemed like a difficult task.

As Roger, Willie Barnes, and Jesse assembled in the West Wing of the White House, coffee was served. Roger had something big on his mind but thought it best to let everyone else speak first. After a few minutes of chitchat, he spoke up. You could tell he was very serious. "Mr. President, I've given a lot of thought to our plans to amend the Constitution. Over this past weekend and for quite some time before that, I thought a lot about changing the Constitution. I know you both have wrestled with these matters as I have. We are trying to make the best decisions for America and her future. I just don't believe America is ready for the changes we hope to get passed.

"For instance the amendment about declaring America a Christian nation, and the amendment recognizing human life at conception, giving every person the same rights—I don't think we will succeed in getting these passed. My reason for saying that is that faith in God is weak or nonexistent in most states. That is how we arrived where we are now, with little or no faith and no respect for human life.

"I do believe there is a way to change the hearts and minds of America, but first let me give you my take on what's left of the American citizen. Every aspect of our lives is inundated with the effects of secular humanism. Secular humanism is a religion accepted by man and inspired by the devil, Satan himself. A void or vacuum is created when mankind denies God, and the unholy void is filled with mankind's design for human life, which is secular humanism. The real everyday reality is that everything boils down to mans-centered attempt to choose what their created purpose in life is. This religion is usually accepted by nonreligious, nonbelieving individuals. Very few are willing to be identified as belonging to an organized religion. The truth is, this is very much a religion, and it is consuming and overwhelming to all its participants or practitioners. At the same time these devastating and enduring characteristics are unbeknownst to the participant involved who actually possesses what I describe simply as a stolen mind. You could say that the absence of truth is a vacuum that is filled with secular humanism.

"Truth is being able to understand what God is telling us. Without God, man's thoughts always lead to a wrong conclusion. For instance, secular humanists grieve over the mistreatment of any animal, but aborting millions of unborn babies is acceptable and beneficial for their concept of mankind's progress. That is how the 'common good' concept was birthed. Also this disease is what guides the Democrats of old into the "modern progressives" of our time. I might add that most of the legislators believe in God but don't really know Him. I believe this failure started with the birth of our country.

"This is what we're up against, but there is a chance." Roger's voice was filled with great excitement and emotion. Both Jesse and Willie were completely captivated by everything Roger was saying. "Jesse, Willie, we have plans to have the army take over the Border Patrol and secure the borders. We've also discussed the air force taking over all the air traffic control towers. If we put our minds to it, the military should be able to take control of many services that are now done by civilians. In America the number of service members on active duty is at the lowest it's ever been. We will need to enlist more servicemen and servicewomen to handle the new duties of the military branches.

"I propose reinstating the draft. That will help immensely with the unemployment problem, but that's not all. That's not the main reason for reinstating the draft. For more years than you or I can recall, there have been many different methods of introducing secular humanism, and many varieties of philosophical studies of truth. These studies have been a mainstay of America's educational system. The introduction starts at a very early age, and before their high school education or college is completed, most of our youths' minds have been stolen or greatly influenced. This has dramatically changed our churches; it has stolen a culture of Americans and deprived citizens of their God-giving liberties. We willingly followed Europe into the abyss.

"Every American military base has classrooms, and the military has always maintained very good teaching facilities. Every person leaving high school, whether man or woman, will be required to serve two years in the military. If a high school graduate goes on to college, their service obligation can be completed through the reserve branches of military service, or after graduating from college. Everybody will be required to serve in a branch of the military service.

"While each recruit will be filling a need, they will be in class learning about American values. We will have classes on American politics; here we will show how legal political action groups combined with unions have had a very adverse effect on America.

"Not many people understand how the progressives got in power; the recruits will learn how this came about. First a need was found, like furnishing wheelchairs for a civic group. This empowered the civic group and gave recognition to the 'progressive party' for caring. Soon this need grew into a national legislative issue that wasn't particularly well known except among the people who were helped. They were indebted to their benefactors. If the opposing party complained, they were looked upon as if they were evil and on the wrong side of an issue. It was the government against the people. This indirectly affected banking, manufacturing, people's credit, and a way of life. The government would provide. Banks didn't need to help a family buy a wheelchair; the manufacturer was selling his product indirectly to the government, and all the family soon became crippled.

"School lunches started with a program to help poor kids have a warm, well-balanced lunch. It grew to three meals a day and children staying at school much longer than needed. Over time, parents—mostly single parents—depended on the help of a caring federal government to raise their children. This allowed the government to be intrusive in every family's life. It was now the duty of the federal government to discipline the children in their care. Over time the parent had to answer to the government on how to raise their child. Most everyone readily accepted this as being best for their children, because they had to. Many Christian families and Christian groups were opposed to the government raising their children, and were forced to homeschool them. The result is that public schools have failed miserably in educating our children and the children have been indoctrinated into a secular belief system.

"We will show that for centuries great philosophers have searched for truth. Their combined minds have made a way for a period of time called the Enlightenment. Here man's truth prevailed; secular humanism started its stranglehold on the civilized world. At about the same time in history the Reformation had begun. To sum up this period, I would merely say that the truth of God was now miraculously available to the masses, so everyone could know God and the truth could spread throughout the world. The truth did spread, but so did the opposition. From both periods of time two different kinds of truth came forward. The result is obvious in every aspect of human life. We all are aware that religion is being taught in many forms in every level of education. This is true except for Christianity, which is still mostly banned. This will be taught as a study called "What Is the Real Truth"—what God has spoken or what man has devised as truth.

I mentioned before that without God, man's thoughts always come to the wrong conclusion. In one conclusion about what truth is, man decided that truth is a consensus of the best minds in the society or in the community. This is how same-sex marriage came about. It seems right to many, but is it based on God's truth? How can you make a society see the difference between man's truth and God's truth? This challenge will be enormous, but over time many minds will understand God's truth. Some of the lost will stay lost in their own delusional folly, but it is their own decision to hear or not to hear. This will eventually change the way churches function in America. I also see that many won't become Christians—they just won't—but they will understand truth, and this will eventually subdue the horrific effects of progressivism. A great majority of progressive followers will continue to follow their own minds. This will be always be true for the ignorant masses who follow an unknown god, secular humanism.

"I know the plan to defund colleges and universities is good for America. I further suggest that the time spent in military classes should earn college credits, credits that can be transferred for a future degree. Most universities and colleges will balk at recognizing classes that are taught in the military. I say that the same classes should be required in both colleges and universities. The graduating student's degree won't be recognized until all requirements are met.

"Looking back at history one can see that after the Dark Ages, man had a clear choice of two journeys: one was secular humanism, and the other was God's way as told in the Bible through Jesus Christ. One was influenced by man, inspiring man to go his own way. The effects of the Enlightenment on civilization will soon deliver the world back to the Dark Ages.

"Men, each year nearly two million young adults graduate high school. What an immediate effect on America this could have. This should turn America a hundred and eighty degrees in the opposite direction. I don't think anyone can stop us, because we are doing exactly as they are doing to us. What is good for the goose is good for the gander. I believe if we change the Constitution to have it profess America as a Christian nation, it will be like forcing our belief system on an unbelieving nation. If we communicate biblical truth, the effects of secularism, and progressivism, America will be as never before. Faith will come naturally, and freedom will reign throughout our land."

Roger stopped talking; he nodded yes, and waited for the president to respond.

Chapter 32

The Ides of March

Tuesday, March 15, 2033

It was five thirty in the morning, and President Hall was by himself in his office drinking coffee. He hadn't slept very well and decided to sit in his office and ponder yesterday's revelations from his vice president, Roger Baker. *This is our only way,* he thought. *We've talked and planned, we've changed this and that, but now this is it. I'm so glad this is coming from Roger. He could go down in history as the man who saved America, and it would be well deserved.* He thought, *I know that all conversations in my office are recorded. I will get Suzy to make a transcript of everything Roger said. It will make history.* He smiled. *The fifteenth of March wasn't very good for Julius Caesar a few centuries ago, but maybe it will be good for us today.*

Jesse's personal cell phone was on his desk, and suddenly it began to ring. At the same time all the phones began to ring. He answered his phone, thinking security could answer the others.

"Hello, this is Jesse Hall. May I help you?" The president didn't bother to look at caller ID to see that it was Luis Parton.

"Sir, Mr. President, this is Luis Parton. I need to meet with you as soon as possible."

"Sure, okay. Come on over. What's going on, Luis?"

Luis replied, "Sir, a federal judge has responded to a request by a large group of American citizens to challenge the constitutionality of your presidency. The judge personally called me about an hour ago. He wanted me to know what was going on before the news came out. I'll give you more details when we meet."

Jesse replied, "Luis, come on over—right now."

After hanging up the phone, President Hall sat in his large leather chair and continued to sip his coffee. *At least on this Ides of March they didn't kill me,* he thought. *Is this too good to be true or is it that for every baby step forward, we take one giant step backward?* As he pondered the new situation, he realized he could be in courts for months trying to get this legal challenge resolved. Then there would be another and then another. *Our efforts could be completely stymied. Do we stop our efforts, hoping that finally the country is awakened, and will not rest until America is headed in the right direction? It could be that America is so weak, this is the final straw. I wonder what kind of chaos would happen if the United States ceased to function as a nation. I'm sure there would be a domino effect, and soon there would be a worldwide catastrophic collapse of governments. Then whoever had the strongest military forces would end up ruling. There would be lots of wars. This may be the biblical end of times anyway, so I should enjoy my coffee and do whatever I can and let whatever happens run its own course. Sometimes we humans are delusional and arrogant enough to think we are running the world. It's really God, and all we can or should do is somehow try to serve Him, so He can be expressed through us. This White House coffee is pretty good. I will have another.*

All the TV stations, the Internet, the newspapers, and every radio station had the same story: is the coup d'état over. It didn't sound very good as it was being presented to the public. It was the story of the century. Just yesterday people had hope, but today there was a heavy burden covering America.

No one had expected such a sudden turn of events; they had come as a total surprise to everyone. America had a constitutional government and President Hall knew full well the ramifications of becoming a president by committee. That was why he had insisted on an election and approval by Congress, but by any stretch of the imagination, these actions were not constitutionally legal. President Hall knew this but didn't expect such a sudden action that could more than likely derail America's last chance for democracy.

Roger Baker came over immediately, and started the meeting with a prayer and said, "Folks, no one expected a hundred-mile-an-hour fastball, but we got one, and it won't be the last. All I can say is that somehow we have to get on base and advance the base runners. If we don't, America is sunk. Let's go around the room and let everybody have a say."

Everyone had something to say but no one really had a solution. Everyone knew that with the way the press was presenting this new dilemma, this new administration would be hard pressed to govern and enact needed changes.

This day wore on in slow motion; it seemed as if a national depression had fallen on America. The *Diagnostic and Statistical Manual* needed to add another classification to cover this new and noticeable affliction that every American citizen was suffering from. The national press was interviewing storeowners and people on the street, trying to get the nation's pulse. It was very obvious that whatever amount of hope had been felt yesterday was now long gone. At the White House it was no different; the staff stayed in conference, but not much was said. It was nearing four thirty in the afternoon when Suzy buzzed President Hall. "Sir, you have a call from Sherry Wilson, Timothy Dawkins's chief of staff."

President Hall answered, "Hello, this is the president speaking."

Sherry Wilson replied, "Mr. President, Speaker Dawkins apologizes for not calling you directly, but he wanted me to convey that Congress will speak to the nation at five o'clock today. Sir, I hope we can get through this mess for the sake of our nation. Also Mr. Dawkins said he would like to talk to you after the newscast."

"Very well. Please have Mr. Dawkins call, or if he can, have him come over. Thanks for letting me know about the news briefing."

Mr. Dawkins got the nod from the cameraman and started. "Good evening, fellow citizens of the United States of America. As a great nation we once again face another crisis. I'm here to share with each of you that this crisis will not deter what must be done to save America. Just three months ago President Wiley and Vice President Gerald Cunningham conspired with Russia, China, Japan, India, Germany, England, and France to unite as one sovereign country. This horrific action could have dissolved this great nation. Not only that, but their unprecedented action would have eventually caused all of Europe and most of the nations in the world to unite as one. Ladies and gentlemen, with the instability throughout the world that presently exists these actions would be catastrophic. There would be unprecedented chaos, which in time would more than likely end by the world being taken over by some great military force. We in America would see foreign military forces streak across our country in our own military machines. It didn't happen, but from that crisis came hope. We still have hope.

"As I speak to you, Congress is drafting a law that will permit President Hall to continue as planned. It will be called the American Recovery Act of Twenty Thirty-Three. This law will give President Hall all the authority needed to continue as planned. This bill will be written in such a way as to withstand any challenges from the Supreme Court. We're planning to have a unanimous vote on this bill by this Friday, March eighteenth.

"One more chance—that's all we're asking for, just one more chance. My question to America is, who gives us one more chance? Is it Congress? No. It's easy to see how many bad bills we approved that caused this nightmare. How about the American citizens? Same answer. You are just like us, a mirror image of the people you have elected to serve you. You wanted as many handouts as we would give you. For decades we expanded the federal government with social programs. We quit balancing the budget. To pay for these extravagances we raised the taxes on the rich, the factories, and the small business. Now they're gone, so I ask you, who is going to give us one more chance?

"When I say we need one more chance, it is also my prayer. Dear God, please give America one more chance. Never mind that we kicked you out of this country many years ago. We slaughtered babies in the womb and sometimes as they were being born. Children are forbidden to pray. There is no restraint on sexual desires. TV and the movies encourage depraved behavior; it is the right of the citizen. No one complains, and the churches are empty and silent. Who is going to give us one more chance?

"Is this the beginning of a new America or is this the end of an old spent nation that's lost its way? There's no place to turn except toward the Lord." With that last comment, Timothy Dawkins ended his speech to the nation by saying, "Fellow citizens of America, I give you this country to do with as you wish. We will respond as God allows us to." With that he left the podium.

Chapter 33

One More Chance

Monday, March 21, 2033

Congress approved the American Recovery Act of Twenty Thirty-Three. The vote was nearly unanimous in both the Senate and House. The newly appointed president was about to address the nation.

"America, I am here to serve. This past Friday, Congress legally validated this presidency. I have more power than any sitting American president ever. I didn't come to Washington for power. When the vote came in, I wasn't very excited. I didn't feel as if I had finally accomplished my lifelong dream. I was terrified. I openly wept. I cried out for God and asked Him for help. This is where I am. This is your new president. May God have mercy on America.

"My first act will be to send envoys to our allies throughout the world. Today, in the real world, not very many countries are on our side or considered true allies. The real truth is that most countries weren't really on our side. Our allies will be assured that America will continue to stand with them against their foes. Other than a few countries, we are pretty well isolated as a nation. I don't see that as a problem. We're open to friendships with other countries, but it will be much different from previous administrations.

"On Friday I was sworn in as president of the United States of America. I swore on the Bible to uphold the Constitution of the United

States. For the life of me, I can't understand how I can swear on God's written word that I would allow the slaughter of unborn babies in their mothers' wombs. Just because we make it a law doesn't make it right, in our sight or God's sight. If the Bible is disregarded for the sake of convenience, then where are we as a nation in the eyes of God?

"Throughout America there are government-supported facilities that do abortions. This can only mean one thing: that what is evil has the appearance of good. The government has tried to remove the shame from abortions. It is common practice in America to kill the not-yet-born baby, and we gladly pay for this horrendous act.

"My second act as president will be to sign into law an immediate suspension on all abortions for the purpose of reviewing as a nation what have we done to our innocent unborn. Congress is in agreement and will write an amendment to the Constitution to protect the unborn, not slaughter them.

"Starting tomorrow, most churches will be open in Washington all day long. I hope the rest of the nation does the same. We are having a funeral for the millions of aborted babies. We will go to the cemetery and have a burial service. I ask that if you've had an abortion, come to the funeral. If you're a husband, mother, father, brother, or sister of an aborted baby, join us and ask for God's mercy. I'm praying that this will help heal many broken hearts. It is God's nature to restore and heal, Let the healing begin."

Many offices were shorthanded; American flags throughout the nation were flown at half-mast, church doors were open, and bells chimed throughout most cities. In every cemetery there were places to have a funeral service for the dead unborn. In the churches the pews were filled with sobbing women, their parents, husbands, and friends. Sometimes the pastors would talk, but usually the focus was ministering to the people.

One more chance: just maybe America will have one more chance.

COMMENTS: jimturnersmail@yahoo.com
www.twentythirty-three.com